THE TRAGEDY OF

ROMEO

Official Student Edition with Annotations

By William Shakespeare

Blackstone Publishing 2019

Table of Contents

Summary

Romeo and Juliet *is a tragedy written by William Shakespeare between 1591-1595, and remains one of his most popular and frequently performed plays. The romance between Romeo and Juliet has become the foundation for many derivative romantic works and established the title characters as the best known of any young lovers in literature. Shakespeare borrowed from other famous tales written earlier in the sixteenth century but expanded upon the plot and characters to create his own version of the famous story.*

The play is set in Verona, Italy, and begins with a scuffle between members the rival families Montague and Capulet. The two families are sworn enemies. The beginning scuffle is between servants of those two houses, and shows that the ill will and animosity of the families runs through the families from the primary members of the family down to their servants.

Capulet, the head of the house of Capulet, has begun receiving interested suitors for his young daughter Juliet. Though her father asks Count Paris, a kinsman of Prince Escalus of Verona, to wait two years for their betrothal, he invites him to attend a Capulet ball. Juliet's mother and nurse try to convince Juliet that a match with Paris would be a good one.

On the Montague side of the family, young Romeo, Montague's son, is explaining his recent depression to cousin Benvolio. Romeo feels heartbroken from his unreturned affection towards a Capulet niece named Rosaline. Despite the danger of sneaking into a Capulet ball, Romeo attends, hoping to woo Rosaline. Instead he sees Juliet and falls in love with her instead. When Juliet's cousin Tybalt finds out Romeo has been at the ball, he has murderous intentions. Juliet's father discourages the violence, not wanting blood spilt at his home.

After their initial meeting, Juliet secretly professes her love for Romeo who is listening at the bottom of her balcony. As he makes his presence known to her, they imagine their futures together and agree to be married the next day by the Friar Laurence. The Friar hopes their union may reconcile the two feuding families.

Tybalt, still enraged, seeks out Romeo and challenges him to a duel, but Romeo declines the fight, believing Tybalt should be his new kinsman. Romeo's friend Mercutio takes on the duel on Romeo's behalf and is mortally wounded. Romeo is wracked with guilt and grief and finally confronts and kills Tybalt. Though Montague argues on his son's behalf, the Prince exiles Romeo from Verona under penalty of death. Romeo hides in Juliet's chamber for the night where the consummate their marriage.

Capulet attempts to marry Juliet to Paris and is dismayed when she refuses. Her pleas to her mother to delay the marriage fall upon deaf ears. Going again to the Friar Laurence for help, she obtains a potion that will make her appear to be in a deathlike coma. The Friar tells Juliet he will send a messenger to inform Romeo and that after she is laid in the family crypt she can run away with Romeo.

The message is tragically not relayed to Romeo and he hears instead of her death from his servant. He buys his own poison and goes to her body, running into Paris at the crypt. In the ensuing battle Romeo kills Paris and then drinks the poison to end his own life.

When Juliet awakens to find her lover dead beside her, she ends her own life by stabbing herself with a dagger. The two rival families meet at the tomb to find the lovers and Paris all death. In their grief they are finally guided towards reconciliation by the Friar Laurence.

Characters in the Play

ROMEO

MONTAGUE, his father

LADY MONTAGUE, his mother

BENVOLIO, their kinsman

ABRAM, a Montague servingman

BALTHASAR, Romeo's servingman

JULIET

CAPULET, her father

LADY CAPULET, her mother

NURSE to Juliet

TYBALT, kinsman to the Capulets

PETRUCHIO, Tybalt's companion

Capulet's Cousin

SAMPSON

GREGORY

PETER

bracketservingmen

Other Servingmen

ESCALUS, Prince of Verona

PARIS, the Prince's kinsman and Juliet's suitor

MERCUTIO, the Prince's kinsman and Romeo's friend

Paris' Page

FRIAR LAWRENCE

FRIAR JOHN

APOTHECARY

Three or four Citizens

Three Musicians

Three Watchmen

THE PROLOGUE

Two households, both alike in dignity

(In fair Verona, where we lay our scene),

From ancient grudge break to new mutiny,

Where civil blood makes civil hands unclean.

From forth the fatal loins of these two foes

A pair of star-crossed lovers take their life;

Whose misadventured piteous overthrows

Doth with their death bury their parents' strife.

The fearful passage of their death-marked love

And the continuance of their parents' rage,

Which, but their children's end, naught could remove,

Is now the two hours' traffic of our stage;

The which, if you with patient ears attend,

What here shall miss, our toil shall strive to mend.

Summary: Shakespeare sets the stage for what will come for Romeo and Juliet. The Chorus informs the audience of the ancient grudge between the two families and calls Romeo and Juliet 'star- crossed lovers'. Are these two lovers just the victim of ill fate? The major theme of this narrative rests on the premise of passionate love, family involvement in marriage, and what two individuals will do to overcome all odds in the name of love. This is the 'fearful passage of their death-marked love', a union beset with ill will from the start, destined for a dire ending.

Glossary:

dignity *rank, or title.*

fatal loins *fateful, unfortunate, offspring.*

star-cross'd lovers *lovers destined to an unhappy fate.*

misadventur'd *unlucky.*

piteous overthrows *their end or death, which arouses or deserves pity or compassion.*

death-mark'd *doomed from the outset; fated.*

two hours traffic *the usual duration of a play.*

Act I

Scene 1: A Public Place

Summary: The first scene opens with a clash on the streets of Verona between servants from the affluent Montague and Capulet households. Although he tries to end the fighting, Benvolio (Romeo's cousin) is brought into the melee by Tybalt, kinsman of the Capulets. The fight quickly intensifies as more citizens become involved leading the heads of both households to arrive on the scene. When Prince Escalus reaches, he stops the riot, forbidding any further occurrences with the threat of death.

Following Escalus dismissal of both sides, Montague and his wife discuss Romeo's recent saddened state with Benvolio and ask him to find out the cause. They exit as Romeo enters in his unhappy state — saddened by the unreturned love by his crush Rosaline. Benvolio instructs Romeo to forget Rosaline by looking for someone else, but Romeo contends he cannot do that.

[Enter Sampson and Gregory armed with swords and bucklers.]

Sampson.
Gregory, o' my word, we'll not carry coals.

Gregory.
No, for then we should be colliers.

Sampson.
I mean, an we be in choler we'll draw.

Gregory.
Ay, while you live, draw your neck out o' the collar.

Sampson.
I strike quickly, being moved.

Gregory.
But thou art not quickly moved to strike.

Sampson.
A dog of the house of Montague moves me.

Gregory.
To move is to stir; and to be valiant is to stand:
therefore, if thou art moved, thou runn'st away.

Sampson.
A dog of that house shall move me to stand:
I will take the wall of any man or maid of
Montague's.

Gregory.
That shows thee a weak slave; for the weakest
goes to the wall.

Sampson.
True; and therefore women, being the weaker
vessels, are ever thrust to the wall: therefore I
will push Montague's men from the wall
and thrust his maids to the wall.

Gregory.
The quarrel is between our masters and us their
men.

Sampson.
'Tis all one, I will show myself a tyrant:
when I have fought with the men I will be cruel
with the maids,
I will cut off their heads.

Gregory.
The heads of the maids?

Sampson.
Ay, the heads of the maids, or their
maidenheads;
take it in what sense thou wilt.

Gregory.
They must take it in sense that feel it.

Sampson.

Me they shall feel while I am able to stand:
and 'tis known I am a pretty piece of flesh.

Gregory.
'Tis well thou art not fish; if thou hadst,
thou hadst been poor-John.--Draw thy tool;
Here comes two of the house of Montagues.

Sampson.
My naked weapon is out: quarrel! I will back
thee.

Gregory.
How! turn thy back and run?

Sampson.
Fear me not.

Gregory.
No, marry; I fear thee!

Sampson.
Let us take the law of our sides; let them begin.

Gregory.
I will frown as I pass by; and let them take it as
they list.

Sampson.
Nay, as they dare. I will bite my thumb at them;
which is disgrace to them if they bear it.

[Enter Abraham and Balthasar.]

Abraham.
Do you bite your thumb at us, sir?

Sampson.
I do bite my thumb, sir.

Abraham.
Do you bite your thumb at us, sir?

Sampson.
Is the law of our side if I say ay?

Gregory.
No.

Sampson.
No, sir, I do not bite my thumb at you, sir; but I
bite my
thumb, sir.

Gregory.
Do you quarrel, sir?

Abraham.
Quarrel, sir! no, sir.

Sampson.
But if you do, sir, am for you: I serve as good a
man as
you.

Abraham.
No better.

Sampson.
Well, sir.

Gregory.
Say better; here comes one of my master's
kinsmen.

Sampson.
Yes, better, sir.

Abraham.
You lie.

Sampson.
Draw, if you be men.--Gregory, remember thy
swashing blow.

[They fight.]

[Enter Benvolio.]

Benvolio.
Part, fools! put up your swords; you know not
what you do.
[Beats down their swords.]

[Enter Tybalt.]

Tybalt.
What, art thou drawn among these heartless

hinds?
Turn thee Benvolio, look upon thy death.

Benvolio.
I do but keep the peace: put up thy sword,
Or manage it to part these men with me.

Tybalt.
What, drawn, and talk of peace! I hate the word
As I hate hell, all Montagues, and thee:
Have at thee, coward!

[They fight.]

[Enter several of both Houses, who join the fray;
then enter
Citizens with clubs.]

1 Citizen.
Clubs, bills, and partisans! strike! beat them
down!
Down with the Capulets! Down with the
Montagues!

[Enter Capulet in his gown, and Lady Capulet.]

Capulet.
What noise is this?--Give me my long sword,
ho!

Lady Capulet.
A crutch, a crutch!--Why call you for a sword?

Capulet.
My sword, I say!--Old Montague is come,
And flourishes his blade in spite of me.

[Enter Montague and his Lady Montague.]

Montague.
Thou villain Capulet!-- Hold me not, let me go.

Lady Montague.
Thou shalt not stir one foot to seek a foe.

[Enter Prince, with Attendants.]

Prince.
Rebellious subjects, enemies to peace,
Profaners of this neighbour-stained steel,--
Will they not hear?--What, ho! you men, you
beasts,
That quench the fire of your pernicious rage
With purple fountains issuing from your veins,--
On pain of torture, from those bloody hands
Throw your mistemper'd weapons to the ground
And hear the sentence of your moved prince.--
Three civil brawls, bred of an airy word,
By thee, old Capulet, and Montague,
Have thrice disturb'd the quiet of our streets;
And made Verona's ancient citizens
Cast by their grave beseeming ornaments,
To wield old partisans, in hands as old,
Canker'd with peace, to part your canker'd hate:
If ever you disturb our streets again,
Your lives shall pay the forfeit of the peace.
For this time, all the rest depart away:--
You, Capulet, shall go along with me;--
And, Montague, come you this afternoon,
To know our farther pleasure in this case,
To old Free town, our common judgment-place.--
Once more, on pain of death, all men depart.

[Exeunt Prince and Attendants; Capulet, Lady
Capulet, Tybalt, Citizens, and Servants.]

Montague.
Who set this ancient quarrel new abroach?--
Speak, nephew, were you by when it began?

Benvolio.
Here were the servants of your adversary
And yours, close fighting ere I did approach:
I drew to part them: in the instant came
The fiery Tybalt, with his sword prepar'd;
Which, as he breath'd defiance to my ears,
He swung about his head, and cut the winds,
Who, nothing hurt withal, hiss'd him in scorn:
While we were interchanging thrusts and blows,
Came more and more, and fought on part and
part,
Till the prince came, who parted either part.

Lady Montague.
O, where is Romeo?--saw you him to-day?--
Right glad I am he was not at this fray.

Benvolio.
Madam, an hour before the worshipp'd sun
Peer'd forth the golden window of the east,
A troubled mind drave me to walk abroad;
Where,--underneath the grove of sycamore
That westward rooteth from the city's side,--
So early walking did I see your son:
Towards him I made; but he was ware of me,
And stole into the covert of the wood:
I, measuring his affections by my own,--
That most are busied when they're most alone,--
Pursu'd my humour, not pursuing his,
And gladly shunn'd who gladly fled from me.

Montague.
Many a morning hath he there been seen,
With tears augmenting the fresh morning's dew,
Adding to clouds more clouds with his deep
sighs:
But all so soon as the all-cheering sun
Should in the farthest east begin to draw
The shady curtains from Aurora's bed,
Away from light steals home my heavy son,
And private in his chamber pens himself;
Shuts up his windows, locks fair daylight out
And makes himself an artificial night:
Black and portentous must this humour prove,
Unless good counsel may the cause remove.

Benvolio.
My noble uncle, do you know the cause?

Montague.
I neither know it nor can learn of him.

Benvolio.
Have you importun'd him by any means?

Montague.
Both by myself and many other friends;
But he, his own affections' counsellor,
Is to himself,--I will not say how true,--

But to himself so secret and so close,
So far from sounding and discovery,
As is the bud bit with an envious worm
Ere he can spread his sweet leaves to the air,
Or dedicate his beauty to the sun.
Could we but learn from whence his sorrows
grow,
We would as willingly give cure as know.

Benvolio.
See, where he comes: so please you step aside;
I'll know his grievance or be much denied.

Montague.
I would thou wert so happy by thy stay
To hear true shrift.--Come, madam, let's away,

[Exeunt Montague and Lady.]

[Enter Romeo.]

Benvolio.
Good morrow, cousin.

Romeo.
Is the day so young?

Benvolio.
But new struck nine.

Romeo.
Ay me! sad hours seem long.
Was that my father that went hence so fast?

Benvolio.
It was.--What sadness lengthens Romeo's hours?

Romeo.
Not having that which, having, makes them
short.

Benvolio.
In love?

Romeo.
Out,--

Benvolio.
Of love?

Romeo.
Out of her favour where I am in love.

Benvolio.
Alas, that love, so gentle in his view,
Should be so tyrannous and rough in proof!

Romeo.
Alas that love, whose view is muffled still,
Should, without eyes, see pathways to his will!--
Where shall we dine?--O me!--What fray was here?
Yet tell me not, for I have heard it all.
Here's much to do with hate, but more with love:--
Why, then, O brawling love! O loving hate!
O anything, of nothing first create!
O heavy lightness! serious vanity!
Mis-shapen chaos of well-seeming forms!
Feather of lead, bright smoke, cold fire, sick health!
Still-waking sleep, that is not what it is!--
This love feel I, that feel no love in this.
Dost thou not laugh?

Benvolio.
No, coz, I rather weep.

Romeo.
Good heart, at what?

Benvolio.
At thy good heart's oppression.

Romeo.
Why, such is love's transgression.--
Griefs of mine own lie heavy in my breast;
Which thou wilt propagate, to have it prest
With more of thine: this love that thou hast shown
Doth add more grief to too much of mine own.
Love is a smoke rais'd with the fume of sighs;
Being purg'd, a fire sparkling in lovers' eyes;

Being vex'd, a sea nourish'd with lovers' tears:
What is it else? a madness most discreet,
A choking gall, and a preserving sweet.--
Farewell, my coz.

[Going.]

Benvolio.
Soft! I will go along:
An if you leave me so, you do me wrong.

Romeo.
Tut! I have lost myself; I am not here:
This is not Romeo, he's some other where.

Benvolio.
Tell me in sadness who is that you love?

Romeo.
What, shall I groan and tell thee?

Benvolio.
Groan! why, no;
But sadly tell me who.

Romeo.
Bid a sick man in sadness make his will,--
Ah, word ill urg'd to one that is so ill!--
In sadness, cousin, I do love a woman.

Benvolio.
I aim'd so near when I suppos'd you lov'd.

Romeo.
A right good markman!--And she's fair I love.

Benvolio.
A right fair mark, fair coz, is soonest hit.

Romeo.
Well, in that hit you miss: she'll not be hit
With Cupid's arrow,--she hath Dian's wit;
And, in strong proof of chastity well arm'd,
From love's weak childish bow she lives unharm'd.
She will not stay the siege of loving terms
Nor bide th' encounter of assailing eyes,
Nor ope her lap to saint-seducing gold:

11

O, she's rich in beauty; only poor
That, when she dies, with beauty dies her store.

Benvolio.
Then she hath sworn that she will still live
chaste?

Romeo.
She hath, and in that sparing makes huge waste;
For beauty, starv'd with her severity,
Cuts beauty off from all posterity.
She is too fair, too wise; wisely too fair,
To merit bliss by making me despair:
She hath forsworn to love; and in that vow
Do I live dead that live to tell it now.

Benvolio.
Be rul'd by me, forget to think of her.

Romeo.
O, teach me how I should forget to think.

Benvolio.
By giving liberty unto thine eyes;
Examine other beauties.

Romeo.
'Tis the way
To call hers, exquisite, in question more:
These happy masks that kiss fair ladies' brows,
Being black, puts us in mind they hide the fair;
He that is strucken blind cannot forget
The precious treasure of his eyesight lost:
Show me a mistress that is passing fair,
What doth her beauty serve but as a note
Where I may read who pass'd that passing fair?
Farewell: thou canst not teach me to forget.

Benvolio.
I'll pay that doctrine, or else die in debt.

[Exeunt]

Glossary:

we'll not carry coals *an old-fashioned saying,
which meant to submit to insults.*

colliers *coal miners.*

draw your neck out of collar *Gregory puns on
the word "draw" here, implying that Sampson
will draw or slip his head out of a hangman's
noose (collar).*

maidenhead *virginity.*

***I will bite my thumb at them, which is a
disgrace to them if they bear it*** *an Italian insult,
a provocative, probably obscene gesture.*

bills *medieval weapons having a hook-shaped
blade with a spike at the back, mounted on a
long staff.*

partisans *broad-bladed weapons with a long
shaft, used especially in the 16th century.*

purple fountains *jets of blood.*

mistemper'd *bad-tempered, angry; here, also
referring to weapons which have been tempered,
or made hard, in blood rather than water.*

moved *angry.*

artificial night *Romeo's behavior is unnatural
(artificial).*

true shrift *confession.*

love so gentle in his view *love, often represented
as Cupid, appears gentle.*

in proof *when actually experienced.*

stay *undergo.*

posterity *Rosaline's celibacy will prevent her
passing on her beauty to her children or
descendants.*

forsworn *promised not to love.*

do I live dead *Romeo regards Rosaline's
decision to remain chaste as a form of living
death.*

Scene II. A Street

Summary: Paris, who is related to the prince, asks Capulet for his daughter Juliet's hand in marriage. Capulet is initially hesitant to give his approval because Juliet is so young. He does Finally agree to the match if Paris can get Juliet's approval.

Capulet invites Paris to a feast that will be held that evening. Capulet sends off the guest list with a servant, who is, unfortunately, illiterate and cannot read the names. He meets Romeo and Benvolio whom he asks for help. Rosaline, Romeo's love interest, is included on the guest list. Romeo decides to go to the feast regardless of the danger of being at the part of Capulet. Benvolio wants Romeo fine another woman at the party to help him forget about Rosaline. Romeo rejects this as a possibility.

[Enter Capulet, Paris, and Servant.]

Capulet.
But Montague is bound as well as I,
In penalty alike; and 'tis not hard, I think,
For men so old as we to keep the peace.

Paris.
Of honourable reckoning are you both;
And pity 'tis you liv'd at odds so long.
But now, my lord, what say you to my suit?

Capulet.
But saying o'er what I have said before:
My child is yet a stranger in the world,
She hath not seen the change of fourteen years;
Let two more summers wither in their pride
Ere we may think her ripe to be a bride.

Paris.
Younger than she are happy mothers made.

Capulet.
And too soon marr'd are those so early made.
The earth hath swallowed all my hopes but she,-

She is the hopeful lady of my earth:
But woo her, gentle Paris, get her heart,
My will to her consent is but a part;
An she agree, within her scope of choice
Lies my consent and fair according voice.
This night I hold an old accustom'd feast,
Whereto I have invited many a guest,
Such as I love; and you among the store,
One more, most welcome, makes my number more.
At my poor house look to behold this night
Earth-treading stars that make dark heaven light:
Such comfort as do lusty young men feel
When well apparell'd April on the heel
Of limping winter treads, even such delight
Among fresh female buds shall you this night
Inherit at my house; hear all, all see,
And like her most whose merit most shall be:
Which, among view of many, mine, being one,
May stand in number, though in reckoning none.
Come, go with me.--Go, sirrah, trudge about
Through fair Verona; find those persons out
Whose names are written there, [gives a paper]
and to them say,
My house and welcome on their pleasure stay.

[Exeunt Capulet and Paris].

Servant.Find them out whose names are written here!
It is written that the shoemaker should meddle with his yard and the tailor with his last, the fisher with his pencil, and the painter with his nets; but I am sent to find those persons whose names are here writ, and can never find what names the writing person hath here writ. I must to the learned:--in good time!

[Enter Benvolio and Romeo.]

Benvolio.
Tut, man, one fire burns out another's burning,
    One pain is lessen'd by another's anguish;
Turn giddy, and be holp by backward turning;

One desperate grief cures with another's languish:
Take thou some new infection to thy eye,
And the rank poison of the old will die.

Romeo.
Your plantain-leaf is excellent for that.

Benvolio.
For what, I pray thee?

Romeo.
For your broken shin.

Benvolio.
Why, Romeo, art thou mad?

Romeo.
Not mad, but bound more than a madman is;
Shut up in prison, kept without my food,
Whipp'd and tormented and--God-den, good fellow.

Servant.
God gi' go-den.--I pray, sir, can you read?

Romeo.
Ay, mine own fortune in my misery.

Servant.
Perhaps you have learned it without book:
but I pray, can you read anything you see?

Romeo.
Ay, If I know the letters and the language.

Servant.
Ye say honestly: rest you merry!

Romeo.
Stay, fellow; I can read. [Reads.]
'Signior Martino and his wife and daughters;
County Anselmo and his beauteous sisters; the
lady widow of Vitruvio; Signior Placentio and
his lovely nieces; Mercutio and his brother
Valentine; mine uncle Capulet, his wife, and
daughters; my fair niece Rosaline; Livia; Signior
Valentio and his cousin Tybalt; Lucio and the

lively Helena.'
A fair assembly. [Gives back the paper]: whither should they come?

Servant.
Up.

Romeo.
Whither?

Servant.
To supper; to our house.

Romeo.
Whose house?

Servant.
My master's.

Romeo.
Indeed I should have ask'd you that before.

Servant.
Now I'll tell you without asking: my master is
the great rich Capulet; and if you be not of the
house of Montagues, I pray, come and crush a
cup of wine. Rest you merry!

[Exit.]

Benvolio.
At this same ancient feast of Capulet's
Sups the fair Rosaline whom thou so lov'st;
With all the admired beauties of Verona.
Go thither; and, with unattainted eye,
Compare her face with some that I shall show,
And I will make thee think thy swan a crow.

Romeo.
When the devout religion of mine eye
    Maintains such falsehood, then turn tears to
fires; And these,--who, often drown'd, could
never die,--
    Transparent heretics, be burnt for liars!
One fairer than my love? the all-seeing sun
Ne'er saw her match since first the world begun.

14

Benvolio.
Tut, you saw her fair, none else being by,
Herself pois'd with herself in either eye:
But in that crystal scales let there be weigh'd
Your lady's love against some other maid
That I will show you shining at this feast,
And she shall scant show well that now shows best.

Romeo.
I'll go along, no such sight to be shown,
But to rejoice in splendour of my own.

[Exeunt]

Glossary:

suit the act of wooing; courtship.

well-apparell'd April clothed or adorned with images of new growth associated with the spring, such as leaves and blossom. Contrast with "limping winter."

sirrah a contemptuous term of address, here used to indicate the difference in social status between Capulet and his servant.

new infection to thy eye Benvolio continues to encourage Romeo to look for another love. Ironically, Romeo and Juliet fall in love at first sight.

plantain leaf the leaf was used to heal cuts and bruises. Romeo replies sarcastically that Benvolio's suggestion of a cure for Romeo's love melancholy would be as effective as applying a plantain leaf.

unattainted unprejudiced.

transparent heretics Romeo says that if he saw another woman more beautiful than Rosaline his tears would turn to fire and burn his eyes as "transparent heretics" for lying.

poised balanced, weighed.

crystal scales Romeo's eyes are like the pans on a set of crystal scales.

Scene III. Room in Capulet's House

Summary: Lady Capulet asks Juliet about her feelings regarding marriage and then tells Juliet of Paris' proposal. When her mother informs Juliet that Paris will be at the feast that evening, Juliet reacts as an obedient daughter, willing to go along with the plans. Juliet's nurse, remembering events from Juliet's childhood, gives a coarser response.

[Enter Lady Capulet, and Nurse.]

Lady Capulet.
Nurse, where's my daughter? call her forth to me.

Nurse.
Now, by my maidenhea,--at twelve year old,--
I bade her come.--What, lamb! what ladybird!--
God forbid!--where's this girl?--what, Juliet!

[Enter Juliet.]

Juliet.
How now, who calls?

Nurse.
Your mother.

Juliet.
Madam, I am here. What is your will?

Lady Capulet.
This is the matter,--Nurse, give leave awhile,
We must talk in secret: nurse, come back again;
I have remember'd me, thou's hear our counsel.
Thou knowest my daughter's of a pretty age.

Nurse.
Faith, I can tell her age unto an hour.

15

Lady Capulet.
She's not fourteen.

Nurse.
I'll lay fourteen of my teeth,--
And yet, to my teen be it spoken, I have but
four,--
She is not fourteen. How long is it now
To Lammas-tide?

Lady Capulet.
A fortnight and odd days.

Nurse.
Even or odd, of all days in the year,
Come Lammas-eve at night shall she be
fourteen.
Susan and she,--God rest all Christian souls!--
Were of an age: well, Susan is with God;
She was too good for me:--but, as I said,
On Lammas-eve at night shall she be fourteen;
That shall she, marry; I remember it well.
'Tis since the earthquake now eleven years;
And she was wean'd,--I never shall forget it--,
Of all the days of the year, upon that day:
For I had then laid wormwood to my dug,
Sitting in the sun under the dove-house wall;
My lord and you were then at Mantua:
Nay, I do bear a brain:--but, as I said,
When it did taste the wormwood on the nipple
Of my dug and felt it bitter, pretty fool,
To see it tetchy, and fall out with the dug!
Shake, quoth the dove-house: 'twas no need, I
trow, To bid me trudge.
And since that time it is eleven years;
For then she could stand alone; nay, by the rood
She could have run and waddled all about;
For even the day before, she broke her brow:
And then my husband,--God be with his soul!
'A was a merry man,--took up the child:
'Yea,' quoth he, 'dost thou fall upon thy face?
Thou wilt fall backward when thou hast more
wit; Wilt thou not, Jule?' and, by my holidame,
The pretty wretch left crying, and said 'Ay:'
To see now how a jest shall come about!

I warrant, an I should live a thousand yeas,
I never should forget it; 'Wilt thou not, Jule?'
quoth he; And, pretty fool, it stinted, and said
'Ay.'

Lady Capulet.
Enough of this; I pray thee hold thy peace.

Nurse.
Yes, madam;--yet I cannot choose but laugh,
To think it should leave crying, and say 'Ay:'
And yet, I warrant, it had upon its brow
A bump as big as a young cockerel's stone;
A parlous knock; and it cried bitterly.
'Yea,' quoth my husband, 'fall'st upon thy face?
Thou wilt fall backward when thou com'st to
age; Wilt thou not, Jule?' it stinted, and said 'Ay.'

Juliet.
And stint thou too, I pray thee, nurse, say I.

Nurse.
Peace, I have done. God mark thee to his grace!
Thou wast the prettiest babe that e'er I nurs'd:
An I might live to see thee married once, I have
my wish.

Lady Capulet.
Marry, that marry is the very theme
I came to talk of.--Tell me, daughter Juliet,
How stands your disposition to be married?

Juliet.
It is an honour that I dream not of.

Nurse.
An honour!--were not I thine only nurse,
I would say thou hadst suck'd wisdom from thy
teat.

Lady Capulet.
Well, think of marriage now: younger than you,
Here in Verona, ladies of esteem,
Are made already mothers: by my count
I was your mother much upon these years
That you are now a maid. Thus, then, in brief;--
The valiant Paris seeks you for his love.

Nurse
A man, young lady! lady, such a man
As all the world--why he's a man of wax.

Lady Capulet.
Verona's summer hath not such a flower.

Nurse.
Nay, he's a flower, in faith, a very flower.

Lady Capulet.
What say you? can you love the gentleman?
This night you shall behold him at our feast;
Read o'er the volume of young Paris' face,
And find delight writ there with beauty's pen;
Examine every married lineament,
And see how one another lends content;
And what obscur'd in this fair volume lies
Find written in the margent of his eyes.
This precious book of love, this unbound lover,
To beautify him, only lacks a cover:
The fish lives in the sea; and 'tis much pride
For fair without the fair within to hide:
That book in many's eyes doth share the glory,
That in gold clasps locks in the golden story;
So shall you share all that he doth possess,
By having him, making yourself no less.

Nurse.
No less! nay, bigger; women grow by men

Lady Capulet.
Speak briefly, can you like of Paris' love?

Juliet.
I'll look to like, if looking liking move;
But no more deep will I endart mine eye
Than your consent gives strength to make it fly.

[Enter a Servant.]

Servant.
Madam, the guests are come, supper served up,
you called, my young lady asked for, the nurse
cursed in the pantry, and everything in
extremity. I must hence to wait; I beseech you,
follow straight.

Lady Capulet.
We follow thee. [Exit Servant.]--
Juliet, the county stays.

Nurse.
Go, girl, seek happy nights to happy days.

[Exeunt]

Glossary:

Lammas-tide *a harvest festival formerly held in England on Aug. 1, when bread baked from the first crop of wheat was consecrated at Mass. The festival is used to symbolize fertility and plentitude, qualities which can be linked to Juliet as a young adolescent.*

laid wormwood to my dug *rubbed wormwood on my nipple: a method of weaning children. The Nurse's role when Juliet was a young child was to act as her wet-nurse and breast-feed Juliet.*

tetchy *touchy; irritable; peevish.*

trow *think.*

by th'rood *an oath: by Christ's cross.*

broke her brow *fell and cut her forehead.*

by my holidame *from the Anglo-Saxon for holiness, here used by the Nurse to mean "holy dame," that is, the Virgin Mary.*

young cockerel's stone *young rooster's testicle.*

stinted *stopped crying.*

disposition *inclination.*

he's a man of wax *he's perfect, without fault, like a wax figure.*

endart *shoot as a dart.*

17

Scene IV. A Street

Summary:

Romeo, Benvolio, Mercutio, and a few others from the Montague household head to the Capulet feast. With their masks hiding their identity, they plan to stay for only one dance.

Romeo continues to be infatuated with Rosaline. Mercutio pokes fun at Romeo for being such a despondent lover. Mercutio then delivers a very inventive Queen Mab speech describing how the fairy delivers dreams to humans as they sleep.

The scene ends with Romeo showing fearful apprehension at what may happen that evening, as if he feels gloom is written in the stars.

[Enter Romeo, Mercutio, Benvolio, with five or six Maskers; Torch-bearers, and others.]

Romeo.
What, shall this speech be spoke for our excuse?
Or shall we on without apology?

Benvolio.
The date is out of such prolixity:
We'll have no Cupid hoodwink'd with a scarf,
Bearing a Tartar's painted bow of lath,
Scaring the ladies like a crow-keeper;
Nor no without-book prologue, faintly spoke
After the prompter, for our entrance:
But, let them measure us by what they will,
We'll measure them a measure, and be gone.

Romeo.
Give me a torch,--I am not for this ambling;
Being but heavy, I will bear the light.

Mercutio.
Nay, gentle Romeo, we must have you dance.

Romeo.
Not I, believe me: you have dancing shoes,

With nimble soles; I have a soul of lead
So stakes me to the ground I cannot move.

Mercutio.
You are a lover; borrow Cupid's wings,
And soar with them above a common bound.

Romeo.
I am too sore enpiercèd with his shaft
To soar with his light feathers; and so bound,
I cannot bound a pitch above dull woe:
Under love's heavy burden do I sink.

Mercutio.
And, to sink in it, should you burden love;
Too great oppression for a tender thing.

Romeo.
Is love a tender thing? it is too rough,
Too rude, too boisterous; and it pricks like thorn.

Mercutio.
If love be rough with you, be rough with love;
Prick love for pricking, and you beat love
down.--
Give me a case to put my visage in: [Putting on
a mask.]
A visard for a visard! what care I
What curious eye doth quote deformities?
Here are the beetle-brows shall blush for me.

Benvolio.
Come, knock and enter; and no sooner in
But every man betake him to his legs.

Romeo.
A torch for me: let wantons, light of heart,
Tickle the senseless rushes with their heels;
For I am proverb'd with a grandsire phrase,--
I'll be a candle-holder and look on,--
The game was ne'er so fair, and I am done.

Mercutio.
Tut, dun's the mouse, the constable's own word:
If thou art dun, we'll draw thee from the mire
Of this--sir-reverence--love, wherein thou

stick'st
Up to the ears.--Come, we burn daylight, ho.

Romeo.
Nay, that's not so.

Mercutio.
I mean, sir, in delay
We waste our lights in vain, like lamps by day.
Take our good meaning, for our judgment sits
Five times in that ere once in our five wits.

Romeo.
And we mean well, in going to this mask;
But 'tis no wit to go.

Mercutio.
Why, may one ask?

Romeo.
I dreamt a dream to-night.

Mercutio.
And so did I.

Romeo.
Well, what was yours?

Mercutio.
That dreamers often lie.

Romeo.
In bed asleep, while they do dream things true.

Mercutio.
O, then, I see Queen Mab hath been with you.
She is the fairies' midwife; and she comes
In shape no bigger than an agate-stone
On the fore-finger of an alderman,
Drawn with a team of little atomies
Athwart men's noses as they lie asleep:
Her waggon-spokes made of long spinners' legs;
The cover, of the wings of grasshoppers;
The traces, of the smallest spider's web;
The collars, of the moonshine's watery beams;
Her whip, of cricket's bone; the lash, of film;
Her waggoner, a small grey-coated gnat,

Not half so big as a round little worm
Prick'd from the lazy finger of a maid:
Her chariot is an empty hazel-nut,
Made by the joiner squirrel or old grub,
Time out o' mind the fairies' coachmakers.
And in this state she gallops night by night
Through lovers' brains, and then they dream of
love; O'er courtiers' knees, that dream on
court'sies straight;
O'er lawyers' fingers, who straight dream on
fees; O'er ladies' lips, who straight on kisses
dream,--
Which oft the angry Mab with blisters plagues,
Because their breaths with sweetmeats tainted
are: Sometime she gallops o'er a courtier's nose,
And then dreams he of smelling out a suit;
And sometime comes she with a tithe-pig's tail,
Tickling a parson's nose as 'a lies asleep,
Then dreams he of another benefice:
Sometime she driveth o'er a soldier's neck,
And then dreams he of cutting foreign throats,
Of breaches, ambuscadoes, Spanish blades,
Of healths five fathom deep; and then anon
Drums in his ear, at which he starts and wakes;
And, being thus frighted, swears a prayer or two,
And sleeps again. This is that very Mab
That plats the manes of horses in the night;
And bakes the elf-locks in foul sluttish hairs,
Which, once untangled, much misfortune bodes:
This is the hag, when maids lie on their backs,
That presses them, and learns them first to bear,
Making them women of good carriage:
This is she,--

Romeo.
Peace, peace, Mercutio, peace,
Thou talk'st of nothing.

Mercutio.
True, I talk of dreams,
Which are the children of an idle brain,
Begot of nothing but vain fantasy;
Which is as thin of substance as the air,
And more inconstant than the wind, who wooes
Even now the frozen bosom of the north,

And, being anger'd, puffs away from thence,
Turning his face to the dew-dropping south.

Benvolio.
This wind you talk of blows us from ourselves:
Supper is done, and we shall come too late.

Romeo.
I fear, too early: for my mind misgives
Some consequence, yet hanging in the stars,
Shall bitterly begin his fearful date
With this night's revels; and expire the term
Of a despised life, clos'd in my breast,
By some vile forfeit of untimely death:
But He that hath the steerage of my course
Direct my sail!--On, lusty gentlemen!

Benvolio.
Strike, drum.

[Exeunt]

Glossary:

hoodwink'd *blindfolded.*

common bound *ordinary limit, with a pun on "bound," as bound to leap about and to be confined.*

a pitch *falconry term used to describe the height from which a bird of prey swoops to seize its prey.*

case *mask.*

quote *note or observe.*

Queen Mab *a fairy queen who controls people's dreams.*

agate stone *a hard, semiprecious stone.*

atomi *creatures as small as atoms.*

long spinners' legs *the legs of the crane fly.*

sweetmeats *any sweet food or delicacy prepared with sugar or honey.*

suit *a petition at court which requires the influence of the courtier for it to be heard, for which he will receive financial reward.*

benefice *an endowed church office providing a living for a vicar, rector, etc.*

ambuscados *ambushes.*

Spanish blades *the best swords were made with Spanish steel.*

vain fantasy *misleading flights of imagination. This is how Mercutio perceives love.*

misgives *feels fear, doubt, or suspicion.*

Scene V. A Hall in Capulet's House.

Summary:

Romeo and his associates reach the Capulet feast. The guests are welcomed by Capulet, who ponders with his cousin how long it hass been since they both participated in a masque. Romeo gets a glimpse of Juliet and immediately falls in love with her. Tybalt identifies Romeo by his voice and sends for his rapier so he can kill him. Capulet insists that Tybalt refrains from a violent conflict with Romeo telling Tybalt about Romeo's good character and the need to have peace at his event.

Romeo and Juliet continue their romantic dialogue and end up kissing. They are interrupted by The Nurse, who sends Juliet to find her mother. After Juliet leaves, Romeo asks the Nurse about Juliet and after finding out that she is a Capulet, realizes the severe consequences of their love. As the feast draws to a close, Romeo leaves with Benvolio and the others. The Nurse then tells Juliet that Romeo is a Montague.

[Musicians waiting. Enter Servants.]

1 Servant.
Where's Potpan, that he helps not to take away?
he shift a trencher! he scrape a trencher!

2 Servant.
When good manners shall lie all in one or two men's
hands, and they unwash'd too, 'tis a foul thing.

1 Servant.
Away with the join-stools, remove the court-cupboard, look
to the plate:--good thou, save me a piece of
marchpane; and as thou loves me, let the porter
let in Susan Grindstone and Nell.--
Antony! and Potpan!

2 Servant.
Ay, boy, ready.

1 Servant.
You are looked for and called for, asked for
and sought for in the great chamber.

2 Servant.
We cannot be here and there too.--Cheerly, boys;
be brisk awhile, and the longer liver take all.

[They retire behind.]

[Enter Capulet, &c. with the Guests the Maskers.]

Capulet.
Welcome, gentlemen! ladies that have their toes
Unplagu'd with corns will have a bout with you.--
Ah ha, my mistresses! which of you all
Will now deny to dance? she that makes dainty,
she, I'll swear hath corns; am I come near you
now? Welcome, gentlemen! I have seen the day
That I have worn a visard; and could tell
A whispering tale in a fair lady's ear,
Such as would please;--'tis gone, 'tis gone, 'tis

gone: You are welcome, gentlemen!--Come,
musicians, play.
A hall--a hall! give room! and foot it, girls.--
[Music plays, and they dance.]
More light, you knaves; and turn the tables up,
And quench the fire, the room is grown too hot.--

Ah, sirrah, this unlook'd-for sport comes well.
Nay, sit, nay, sit, good cousin Capulet;
For you and I are past our dancing days;
How long is't now since last yourself and I
Were in a mask?

2 Capulet.
By'r Lady, thirty years.

Capulet.
What, man! 'tis not so much, 'tis not so much:
'Tis since the nuptial of Lucentio,
Come Pentecost as quickly as it will,
Some five-and-twenty years; and then we
mask'd.

2 Capulet.
'Tis more, 'tis more: his son is elder, sir;
His son is thirty.

Capulet.
Will you tell me that?
His son was but a ward two years ago.

Romeo.
What lady is that, which doth enrich the hand
Of yonder knight?

Servant.
I know not, sir.

Romeo.
O, she doth teach the torches to burn bright!
It seems she hangs upon the cheek of night
Like a rich jewel in an Ethiop's ear;
Beauty too rich for use, for earth too dear!
So shows a snowy dove trooping with crows
As yonder lady o'er her fellows shows.
The measure done, I'll watch her place of stand

And, touching hers, make blessed my rude hand.
Did my heart love till now? forswear it, sight!
For I ne'er saw true beauty till this night.

Tybalt.
This, by his voice, should be a Montague.--
Fetch me my rapier, boy:--what, dares the slave
Come hither, cover'd with an antic face,
To fleer and scorn at our solemnity?
Now, by the stock and honour of my kin,
To strike him dead I hold it not a sin.

Capulet.
Why, how now, kinsman! wherefore storm you
so?

Tybalt.
Uncle, this is a Montague, our foe;
A villain, that is hither come in spite,
To scorn at our solemnity this night.

Capulet.
Young Romeo, is it?

Tybalt.
'Tis he, that villain, Romeo.

Capulet.
Content thee, gentle coz, let him alone,
He bears him like a portly gentleman;
And, to say truth, Verona brags of him
To be a virtuous and well-govern'd youth:
I would not for the wealth of all the town
Here in my house do him disparagement:
Therefore be patient, take no note of him,--
It is my will; the which if thou respect,
Show a fair presence and put off these frowns,
An ill-beseeming semblance for a feast.

Tybalt.
It fits, when such a villain is a guest:
I'll not endure him.

Capulet.
He shall be endur'd:
What, goodman boy!--I say he shall;--go to;
Am I the master here, or you? go to.

You'll not endure him!--God shall mend my
soul, You'll make a mutiny among my guests!
You will set cock-a-hoop! you'll be the man!

Tybalt.
Why, uncle, 'tis a shame.

Capulet.
Go to, go to!
You are a saucy boy. Is't so, indeed?--
This trick may chance to scathe you,--I know
what: You must contrary me! marry, 'tis time.--
Well said, my hearts!--You are a princox; go:
Be quiet, or--More light, more light!--For
shame! I'll make you quiet. What!--cheerly, my
hearts.

Tybalt.
Patience perforce with wilful choler meeting
Makes my flesh tremble in their different
greeting.
I will withdraw: but this intrusion shall,
Now seeming sweet, convert to bitter gall.

[Exit.]

Romeo.
[To Juliet.] If I profane with my unworthiest
hand
   This holy shrine, the gentle fine is this,--
My lips, two blushing pilgrims, ready stand
   To smooth that rough touch with a tender kiss.

Juliet.
Good pilgrim, you do wrong your hand too
much, Which mannerly devotion shows in this;
For saints have hands that pilgrims' hands do
touch, And palm to palm is holy palmers' kiss.

Romeo.
Have not saints lips, and holy palmers too?

Juliet.
Ay, pilgrim, lips that they must use in prayer.

Romeo.

O, then, dear saint, let lips do what hands do;
They pray, grant thou, lest faith turn to despair.

Juliet.
Saints do not move, though grant for prayers'
sake.

Romeo.
Then move not while my prayer's effect I take.
Thus from my lips, by thine my sin is purg'd.
[Kissing her.]

Juliet.
Then have my lips the sin that they have took.

Romeo.
Sin from my lips? O trespass sweetly urg'd!
Give me my sin again.

Juliet.
You kiss by the book.

Nurse.
Madam, your mother craves a word with you.

Romeo.
What is her mother?

Nurse.
Marry, bachelor,
Her mother is the lady of the house.
And a good lady, and a wise and virtuous:
I nurs'd her daughter that you talk'd withal;
I tell you, he that can lay hold of her
Shall have the chinks.

Romeo.
Is she a Capulet?
O dear account! my life is my foe's debt.

Benvolio.
Away, be gone; the sport is at the best.

Romeo.
Ay, so I fear; the more is my unrest.

Capulet.
Nay, gentlemen, prepare not to be gone;

We have a trifling foolish banquet towards.--
Is it e'en so? why then, I thank you all;
I thank you, honest gentlemen; good-night.--
More torches here!--Come on then, let's to bed.
Ah, sirrah [to 2 Capulet], by my fay, it waxes
late; I'll to my rest.

[Exeunt all but Juliet and Nurse.]

Juliet.
Come hither, nurse. What is yond gentleman?

Nurse.
The son and heir of old Tiberio.

Juliet.
What's he that now is going out of door?

Nurse.
Marry, that, I think, be young Petruchio.

Juliet.
What's he that follows there, that would not
dance?

Nurse.
I know not.

Juliet.
Go ask his name: if he be married,
My grave is like to be my wedding-bed

Nurse.
His name is Romeo, and a Montague;
The only son of your great enemy.

Juliet.
My only love sprung from my only hate!
Too early seen unknown, and known too late!
Prodigious birth of love it is to me,
That I must love a loathed enemy.

Nurse.
What's this? What's this?

Juliet.
A rhyme I learn'd even now
Of one I danc'd withal.

[One calls within, 'Juliet.']

Nurse.
Anon, anon!
Come, let's away; the strangers all are gone.

[Exit]
[Enter Chorus.]

Chorus.
Now old desire doth in his deathbed lie,
    And young affection gapes to be his heir;
That fair for which love groan'd for, and would
die,With tender Juliet match'd, is now not fair.
Now Romeo is belov'd, and loves again,
    Alike bewitched by the charm of looks;
But to his foe suppos'd he must complain,
    And she steal love's sweet bait from fearful
hooks:
Being held a foe, he may not have access
    To breathe such vows as lovers us'd to swear;
And she as much in love, her means much less
    To meet her new beloved anywhere:
But passion lends them power, time means, to
meet,
    Tempering extremities with extreme sweet.

[Exeunt]

Glossary:

trencher *a wooden board or platter on which to
carve or serve meat.*

marchpane *marzipan, a confection of ground
almonds, sugar, and egg white made into a paste
and variously shaped and colored.*

visor *mask.*

Pentecost *a religious festival, the seventh
Sunday after Easter.*

antic face *Romeo's face is still covered by his
mask.*

to fleer *to laugh derisively (at); sneer or jeer
(at).*

portly *dignified or well-mannered.*

disparagement *disrespect.*

an ill-beseeming semblance *an unfitting or
inappropriate outward appearance or aspect.*

set cock-a-hoop *be boastful or conceited.
Capulet is concerned that Tybalt's anger and
lack of restraint will spoil the feast.*

princox *a coxcomb; fop. Capulet is keen to
belittle Tybalt and force him to submit to his will
as head of the household.*

bitt'rest gall *bitter feeling; rancor. Gall is
another name for bile, one of the bodily humors
(that is, bodily fluids thought to be responsible
for one's health and disposition).*

holy palmers' kiss *a palmer is a pilgrim who
carried a palm leaf to signify the making of a
pilgrimage to the Holy Land. For Romeo, love is
likened to a religious quest.*

you kiss by th'book *that is, according to
convention.*

marry *an exclamation of surprise. "Marry" is a
respelling of (the Virgin) "Mary."*

the chinks *plenty of cash.*

fay *faith: used in oaths as here.*

prodigious *both wonderful and portentous.*

Act II

Summary:

24

Act II opens with a chorus in sonnet form emphasizing two key points: how Romeo is impacted by meeting Juliet and the problems the lovers will face as members of two rival families.

Chorus

Now old desire doth in his deathbed lie,
And young affection gapes to be his heir.
That fair for which love groaned for and would die,
With tender Juliet matched, is now not fair.
Now Romeo is beloved and loves again,
Alike bewitchèd by the charm of looks,
But to his foe supposed he must complain,
And she steal love's sweet bait from fearful hooks.
Being held a foe, he may not have access
To breathe such vows as lovers use to swear,
And she as much in love, her means much less
To meet her new belovèd anywhere.
But passion lends them power, time means, to meet,
Temp'ring extremities with extreme sweet.

Scene I. An open place adjoining Capulet's Garden.

Summary:

This scene occurs outside the Capulet orchard. Romeo longs to see Juliet again after falling in love with her at first sight at the Capulet masquerade ball. He hops over the orchard wall when he hears Mercutio and Benvolio in the near distance. His friends do not know that Romeo has met and fallen in love with Juliet. Mercutio clowns with Romeo by teasing him about Rosaline's enticing beauty. Romeo continues hiding. Benvolio convinces Mercutio to leave the scene because he knows Romeo loves solitude.

[Enter Romeo.]

Romeo.
Can I go forward when my heart is here?
Turn back, dull earth, and find thy centre out.

[He climbs the wall and leaps down within it.]

[Enter Benvolio and Mercutio.]

Benvolio.
Romeo! my cousin Romeo!

Mercutio.
He is wise; And, on my life, hath stol'n him home to bed.

Benvolio.
He ran this way, and leap'd this orchard wall:
Call, good Mercutio.

Mercutio.
Nay, I'll conjure too.--
Romeo! humours! madman! passion! lover!
Appear thou in the likeness of a sigh:
Speak but one rhyme, and I am satisfied;
Cry but 'Ah me!' pronounce but Love and dove;
Speak to my gossip Venus one fair word,
One nickname for her purblind son and heir,
Young auburn Cupid, he that shot so trim
When King Cophetua lov'd the beggar-maid!--
He heareth not, he stirreth not, he moveth not;
The ape is dead, and I must conjure him.--
I conjure thee by Rosaline's bright eyes,
By her high forehead and her scarlet lip,
By her fine foot, straight leg, and quivering thigh, And the demesnes that there adjacent lie,
That in thy likeness thou appear to us!

Benvolio.
An if he hear thee, thou wilt anger him.

Mercutio.
This cannot anger him: 'twould anger him
To raise a spirit in his mistress' circle,
Of some strange nature, letting it there stand
Till she had laid it, and conjur'd it down;
That were some spite: my invocation

25

Is fair and honest, and, in his mistress' name,
I conjure only but to raise up him.

Benvolio.
Come, he hath hid himself among these trees,
To be consorted with the humorous night:
Blind is his love, and best befits the dark.

Mercutio.
If love be blind, love cannot hit the mark.
Now will he sit under a medlar tree,
And wish his mistress were that kind of fruit
As maids call medlars when they laugh alone.--
Romeo, good night.--I'll to my truckle-bed;
This field-bed is too cold for me to sleep:
Come, shall we go?

Benvolio.
Go then; for 'tis in vain
To seek him here that means not to be found.

[Exeunt]

Glossary:

dull earth Romeo's description of himself.

conjure to summon a demon or spirit as by a magic spell. Mercutio attempts to raise or draw Romeo from his hiding place.

when King . . . lov'd the beggar maid a 16th-century ballad.

the ape is dead Romeo is described as a performing monkey who is playing dead and will not respond to Mercutio's conjuration.

demesnes a region or domain. Here Mercutio uses it to refer bawdily to the female genitalia.

to raise a spirit in his mistresses circle Mercutio puns on circle as both the magician's magic circle and the female genitalia.

consorted associated with.

medlars small, brown, apple-like fruit.

open-arse slang term for a medlar; "arse" is the buttocks.

poperin pear Mercutio compares the pear with the shape of the male genitals and puns on the name: pop-her-in.

truckle-bed a low bed on small wheels or casters, that can be rolled under another bed when not in use.

field-bed bed upon the ground.

Scene II. Capulet's Garden.

Summary:

Romeo stands in the darkness underneath Juliet's bedroom window. Juliet comes out onto the balcony and believing she is alone, divulges in a monologue her love for Romeo. She anguishes over the grudge between their two families and the difficulties the dispute presents. Romeo stands listening and as Juliet beckons him to shed his Montague name, he steps from the shadows and exclaims, "call me but love."

After the two exchange in a monologue expressing their devotion, the Nurse calls Juliet from the balcony. Juliet departs, but comes back momentarily. They decide to marry. Juliet tells Romeo she will send him a messenger the next day so he can reveal the wedding plans he has made. The scene ends as day breaks and Romeo leaves to get the guidance of Friar Laurence.

[Enter Romeo.]

Romeo.
He jests at scars that never felt a wound.--
[Juliet appears above at a window.]
But soft! what light through yonder window breaks?
It is the east, and Juliet is the sun!--
Arise, fair sun, and kill the envious moon,
Who is already sick and pale with grief,

That thou her maid art far more fair than she:
Be not her maid, since she is envious;
Her vestal livery is but sick and green,
And none but fools do wear it; cast it off.--
It is my lady; O, it is my love!
O, that she knew she were!--
She speaks, yet she says nothing: what of that?
Her eye discourses, I will answer it.--
I am too bold, 'tis not to me she speaks:
Two of the fairest stars in all the heaven,
Having some business, do entreat her eyes
To twinkle in their spheres till they return.
What if her eyes were there, they in her head?
The brightness of her cheek would shame those
stars, As daylight doth a lamp; her eyes in
heaven Would through the airy region stream so
bright That birds would sing and think it were
not night.--
See how she leans her cheek upon her hand!
O that I were a glove upon that hand,
That I might touch that cheek!

Juliet.
Ah me!

Romeo.
She speaks:--
O, speak again, bright angel! for thou art
As glorious to this night, being o'er my head,
As is a winged messenger of heaven
Unto the white-upturned wondering eyes
Of mortals that fall back to gaze on him
When he bestrides the lazy-pacing clouds
And sails upon the bosom of the air.

Juliet.
O Romeo, Romeo! wherefore art thou Romeo?
Deny thy father and refuse thy name;
Or, if thou wilt not, be but sworn my love,
And I'll no longer be a Capulet.

Romeo.
[Aside.] Shall I hear more, or shall I speak at
this?

Juliet.
'Tis but thy name that is my enemy;--
Thou art thyself, though not a Montague.
What's Montague? It is nor hand, nor foot,
Nor arm, nor face, nor any other part
Belonging to a man. O, be some other name!
What's in a name? that which we call a rose
By any other name would smell as sweet;
So Romeo would, were he not Romeo call'd,
Retain that dear perfection which he owes
Without that title:--Romeo, doff thy name;
And for that name, which is no part of thee,
Take all myself.

Romeo.
I take thee at thy word:
Call me but love, and I'll be new baptiz'd;
Henceforth I never will be Romeo.

Juliet.
What man art thou that, thus bescreen'd in night,
So stumblest on my counsel?

Romeo.
By a name
I know not how to tell thee who I am:
My name, dear saint, is hateful to myself,
Because it is an enemy to thee.
Had I it written, I would tear the word.

Juliet.
My ears have yet not drunk a hundred words
Of that tongue's utterance, yet I know the sound;
Art thou not Romeo, and a Montague?

Romeo.
Neither, fair saint, if either thee dislike.

Juliet.
How cam'st thou hither, tell me, and wherefore?
The orchard walls are high and hard to climb;
And the place death, considering who thou art,
If any of my kinsmen find thee here.

Romeo.
With love's light wings did I o'erperch these

27

walls;
For stony limits cannot hold love out:
And what love can do, that dares love attempt;
Therefore thy kinsmen are no let to me.

Juliet.
If they do see thee, they will murder thee.

Romeo.
Alack, there lies more peril in thine eye
Than twenty of their swords: look thou but
sweet, And I am proof against their enmity.

Juliet.
I would not for the world they saw thee here.

Romeo.
I have night's cloak to hide me from their sight;
And, but thou love me, let them find me here.
My life were better ended by their hate
Than death prorogued, wanting of thy love.

Juliet.
By whose direction found'st thou out this place?

Romeo.
By love, that first did prompt me to enquire;
He lent me counsel, and I lent him eyes.
I am no pilot; yet, wert thou as far
As that vast shore wash'd with the furthest sea,
I would adventure for such merchandise.

Juliet.
Thou knowest the mask of night is on my face;
Else would a maiden blush bepaint my cheek
For that which thou hast heard me speak to-
night.
Fain would I dwell on form,fain, fain deny
What I have spoke; but farewell compliment!
Dost thou love me, I know thou wilt say Ay;
And I will take thy word: yet, if thou swear'st,
Thou mayst prove false; at lovers' perjuries,
They say Jove laughs. O gentle Romeo,
If thou dost love, pronounce it faithfully:
Or if thou thinkest I am too quickly won,
I'll frown, and be perverse, and say thee nay,

So thou wilt woo: but else, not for the world.
In truth, fair Montague, I am too fond;
And therefore thou mayst think my 'haviour
light:
But trust me, gentleman, I'll prove more true
Than those that have more cunning to be
strange.
I should have been more strange, I must confess,
But that thou overheard'st, ere I was 'ware,
My true-love passion: therefore pardon me;
And not impute this yielding to light love,
Which the dark night hath so discovered.

Romeo.
Lady, by yonder blessed moon I swear,
That tips with silver all these fruit-tree tops,--

Juliet.
O, swear not by the moon, the inconstant moon,
That monthly changes in her circled orb,
Lest that thy love prove likewise variable.

Romeo.
What shall I swear by?

Juliet.
Do not swear at all;
Or if thou wilt, swear by thy gracious self,
Which is the god of my idolatry,
And I'll believe thee.

Romeo.
If my heart's dear love,--

Juliet.
Well, do not swear: although I joy in thee,
I have no joy of this contract to-night;
It is too rash, too unadvis'd, too sudden;
Too like the lightning, which doth cease to be
Ere one can say It lightens. Sweet, good night!
This bud of love, by summer's ripening breath,
May prove a beauteous flower when next we
meet.
Good night, good night! as sweet repose and rest
Come to thy heart as that within my breast!

Romeo.

O, wilt thou leave me so unsatisfied?

Juliet.

What satisfaction canst thou have to-night?

Romeo.

The exchange of thy love's faithful vow for mine.

Juliet.

I gave thee mine before thou didst request it;
And yet I would it were to give again.

Romeo.

Would'st thou withdraw it? for what purpose, love?

Juliet.

But to be frank and give it thee again.
And yet I wish but for the thing I have;
My bounty is as boundless as the sea,
My love as deep; the more I give to thee,
The more I have, for both are infinite.
I hear some noise within: dear love, adieu!--
[Nurse calls within.]
Anon, good nurse!--Sweet Montague, be true.
Stay but a little, I will come again.

[Exit.]

Romeo.

O blessed, blessed night! I am afeard,
Being in night, all this is but a dream,
Too flattering-sweet to be substantial.

[Enter Juliet above.]

Juliet.

Three words, dear Romeo, and good night indeed.
If that thy bent of love be honourable,
Thy purpose marriage, send me word to-morrow,
By one that I'll procure to come to thee,
Where and what time thou wilt perform the rite;

And all my fortunes at thy foot I'll lay
And follow thee, my lord, throughout the world.

Nurse.

[Within.] Madam!

Juliet.

I come anon.-- But if thou meanest not well,
I do beseech thee,--

Nurse.

[Within.] Madam!

Juliet.

By-and-by I come:--
To cease thy suit and leave me to my grief:
To-morrow will I send.

Romeo.

So thrive my soul,--

Juliet.

A thousand times good night!

[Exit.]

Romeo.

A thousand times the worse, to want thy light!--
Love goes toward love as schoolboys from their books;
But love from love, towards school with heavy looks.

[Retirong slowly.]

[Re-enter Juliet, above.]

Juliet.

Hist! Romeo, hist!--O for a falconer's voice
To lure this tassel-gentle back again!
Bondage is hoarse and may not speak aloud;
Else would I tear the cave where Echo lies,
And make her airy tongue more hoarse than mine
With repetition of my Romeo's name.

Romeo.

It is my soul that calls upon my name:

How silver-sweet sound lovers' tongues by night,
Like softest music to attending ears!

Juliet.
Romeo!

Romeo.
My dear?

Juliet.
At what o'clock to-morrow
Shall I send to thee?

Romeo.
At the hour of nine.

Juliet.
I will not fail: 'tis twenty years till then.
I have forgot why I did call thee back.

Romeo.
Let me stand here till thou remember it.

Juliet.
I shall forget, to have thee still stand there,
Remembering how I love thy company.

Romeo.
And I'll still stay, to have thee still forget,
Forgetting any other home but this.

Juliet.
'Tis almost morning; I would have thee gone:
And yet no farther than a wanton's bird;
That lets it hop a little from her hand,
Like a poor prisoner in his twisted gyves,
And with a silk thread plucks it back again,
So loving-jealous of his liberty.

Romeo.
I would I were thy bird.

Juliet.
Sweet, so would I:
Yet I should kill thee with much cherishing.
Good night, good night! parting is such sweet sorrow
That I shall say good night till it be morrow.

[Exit.]

Romeo.
Sleep dwell upon thine eyes, peace in thy breast!--
Would I were sleep and peace, so sweet to rest!
Hence will I to my ghostly father's cell,
His help to crave and my dear hap to tell.

[Exeunt]

Glossary:

her vestal livery *chaste appearance or virginal dress.*

sick and green *pale and sickly. Green was the color associated with maids.*

wherefore *why?*

doff *discard.*

enmity *hatred; hostility.*

prorogued *delayed; postponed.*

I am no pilot . . . should adventure for such merchandise *Romeo describes himself as a merchant venturer, one who would make risky voyages to be with Juliet.*

perjuries *the breaking of promises.*

Jove *king of the Roman gods.*

fond *tender and affectionate; loving; sometimes, affectionate in a foolish or overly indulgent way.*

strange *reserved, aloof.*

the god of my idolatry *the object of my excessive devotion.*

tassel-gentle *from "tiercel," a falconry term for a male hawk, especially the male peregrine.*

bondage is hoarse and may not speak aloud at home, Juliet is under her father's strict discipline and must whisper as though she is hoarse to avoid detection.

a wanton's bird that is, the pet of an undisciplined, spoiled child.

hap good luck or news.

Scene III. Friar Lawrence's Cell

Summary:

Romeo gets to Friar Laurence's cell by dawn. The Friar is gathering flowers and herbs while he ruminates on their abilities to both heal and poison. Romeo tells the Friar about his love for Juliet and asks if the Friar can marry the two of them later that day. The Friar is astonished and worried about how fast Romeo has transferred his love from Rosaline to Juliet, but does agree to help the young couple, hoping their marriage might ease the conflict between the two families.

[Enter Friar Lawrence with a basket.]

Friar.
The grey-ey'd morn smiles on the frowning night,
Chequering the eastern clouds with streaks of light;
And flecked darkness like a drunkard reels
From forth day's path and Titan's fiery wheels:
Non, ere the sun advance his burning eye,
The day to cheer and night's dank dew to dry,
I must up-fill this osier cage of ours
With baleful weeds and precious-juiced flowers.
The earth, that's nature's mother, is her tomb;
What is her burying grave, that is her womb:
And from her womb children of divers kind
We sucking on her natural bosom find;
Many for many virtues excellent,
None but for some, and yet all different.
O, mickle is the powerful grace that lies
In plants, herbs, stones, and their true qualities:

For naught so vile that on the earth doth live
But to the earth some special good doth give;
Nor aught so good but, strain'd from that fair use,
Revolts from true birth, stumbling on abuse:
Virtue itself turns vice, being misapplied;
And vice sometimes by action dignified.
Within the infant rind of this small flower
Poison hath residence, and medicine power:
For this, being smelt, with that part cheers each part;
Being tasted, slays all senses with the heart.
Two such opposed kings encamp them still
In man as well as herbs,--grace and rude will;
And where the worser is predominant,
Full soon the canker death eats up that plant.

[Enter Romeo.]

Romeo.
Good morrow, father!

Friar.
Benedicite!
What early tongue so sweet saluteth me?--
Young son, it argues a distemper'd head
So soon to bid good morrow to thy bed:
Care keeps his watch in every old man's eye,
And where care lodges sleep will never lie;
But where unbruised youth with unstuff'd brain
Doth couch his limbs, there golden sleep doth reign:
Therefore thy earliness doth me assure
Thou art uprous'd with some distemperature;
Or if not so, then here I hit it right,--
Our Romeo hath not been in bed to-night.

Romeo.
That last is true; the sweeter rest was mine.

Friar.
God pardon sin! wast thou with Rosaline?

Romeo.
With Rosaline, my ghostly father? no;
I have forgot that name, and that name's woe.

31

Friar.
That's my good son: but where hast thou been
then?

Romeo.
I'll tell thee ere thou ask it me again.
I have been feasting with mine enemy;
Where, on a sudden, one hath wounded me
That's by me wounded. Both our remedies
Within thy help and holy physic lies;
I bear no hatred, blessed man; for, lo,
My intercession likewise steads my foe.

Friar.
Be plain, good son, and homely in thy drift;
Riddling confession finds but riddling shrift.

Romeo.
Then plainly know my heart's dear love is set
On the fair daughter of rich Capulet:
As mine on hers, so hers is set on mine;
And all combin'd, save what thou must combine
By holy marriage: when, and where, and how
We met, we woo'd, and made exchange of vow,
I'll tell thee as we pass; but this I pray,
That thou consent to marry us to-day.

Friar.
Holy Saint Francis! what a change is here!
Is Rosaline, that thou didst love so dear,
So soon forsaken? young men's love, then, lies
Not truly in their hearts, but in their eyes.
Jesu Maria, what a deal of brine
Hath wash'd thy sallow cheeks for Rosaline!
How much salt water thrown away in waste,
To season love, that of it doth not taste!
The sun not yet thy sighs from heaven clears,
Thy old groans ring yet in mine ancient ears;
Lo, here upon thy cheek the stain doth sit
Of an old tear that is not wash'd off yet:
If e'er thou wast thyself, and these woes thine,
Thou and these woes were all for Rosaline;
And art thou chang'd? Pronounce this sentence
then,--

Women may fall, when there's no strength in
men.

Romeo.
Thou chidd'st me oft for loving Rosaline.

Friar.
For doting, not for loving, pupil mine.

Romeo.
And bad'st me bury love.

Friar.
Not in a grave
To lay one in, another out to have.

Romeo.
I pray thee chide not: she whom I love now
Doth grace for grace and love for love allow;
The other did not so.

Friar.
O, she knew well
Thy love did read by rote, that could not spell.
But come, young waverer, come go with me,
In one respect I'll thy assistant be;
For this alliance may so happy prove,
To turn your households' rancour to pure love.

Romeo.
O, let us hence; I stand on sudden haste.

Friar.
Wisely, and slow; they stumble that run fast.

[Exeunt]

Glossary:

advance raise.

osier cage basket made from willow.

baleful harmful or poisonous.

virtues qualities.

mickle much or great.

residence *the place in which a person or thing resides.*

benedicite *Latin for "bless you!"*

distemperature *a disordered condition, especially of the body or the mind.*

holy physic *spiritual remedy.*

intercession *prayers and petitions.*

steads *is of benefit to.*

riddling *puzzling or enigmatic.*

shrift *confession.*

brine *salt water; that is, tears.*

by rote *by memory alone, without understanding or thought.*

rancour *a continuing and bitter hate or ill will.*

Scene IV. A Street

Summary:

The next morning after the Capulet masquerade, Mercutio and Benvolio look for Romeo. Mercutio thinks Romeo's disappearance is due to his love for the cold hearted Rosaline. Benvolio finds out that Tybalt has challenged Romeo to a duel. Mercutio finds the idea of a duel between Romeo the romantic and Tybalt, the fashionable "Prince of Cats" humorous. When Romeo does arrive, he and Mercutio exchange in a long series of back and forth jesting.

The Nurse enters with her servant, Peter, seeking out Romeo. Mercutio annoys the nurse with his quick, sharp jeering. After Mercutio leaves with Benvolio, Romeo tells the Nurse to have Juliet meet him at Friar Laurence's cell at

2 p.m. that afternoon so they can get married. The Nurse is told to get a rope ladder from Romeo so he can climb to Juliet's window and celebrate their wedding night.

[Enter Benvolio and Mercutio.]

Mercutio.
Where the devil should this Romeo be?--
Came he not home to-night?

Benvolio.
Not to his father's; I spoke with his man.

Mercutio.
Ah, that same pale hard-hearted wench, that Rosaline,
Torments him so that he will sure run mad.

Benvolio.
Tybalt, the kinsman to old Capulet,
Hath sent a letter to his father's house.

Mercutio.
A challenge, on my life.

Benvolio.
Romeo will answer it.

Mercutio.
Any man that can write may answer a letter.

Benvolio.
Nay, he will answer the letter's master, how he dares, being dared.

Mercutio.
Alas, poor Romeo, he is already dead! stabbed with a white wench's black eye; shot through the ear with a love song; the very
pin of his heart cleft with the blind bow-boy's butt-shaft: and is he a man to encounter Tybalt?

Benvolio.
Why, what is Tybalt?

Mercutio.
More than prince of cats, I can tell you. O, he's

33

the courageous captain of compliments. He fights as you sing prick-song--keeps time, distance, and proportion; rests me his minim rest, one, two, and the third in your bosom: the very butcher of a silk button, a duellist, a duellist; a gentleman of the very first house,--of the first and second cause: ah, the immortal passado! the punto reverso! the hay.--

Benvolio.
The what?

Mercutio.
The pox of such antic, lisping, affecting fantasticoes; these new tuners of accents!--'By Jesu, a very good blade!--a very tall man!--a very good whore!'--Why, is not this a lamentable thing, grandsire, that we should be thus afflicted with these strange flies, these fashion-mongers, these pardonnez-moi's, who stand so much on the new form that they cannot sit at ease on the old bench? O, their bons, their bons!

Benvolio.
Here comes Romeo, here comes Romeo!

Mercutio.
Without his roe, like a dried herring.--O flesh, flesh, how art thou fishified!--Now is he for the numbers that Petrarch flowed in: Laura, to his lady, was but a kitchen wench,--marry, she had a better love to be-rhyme her; Dido, a dowdy; Cleopatra, a gypsy; Helen and Hero, hildings and harlots; Thisbe, a gray eye or so, but not to the purpose,--

[Enter Romeo.]

Signior Romeo, bon jour! there's a French salutation to your French slop. You gave us the counterfeit fairly last night.

Romeo.
Good morrow to you both. What counterfeit did I give you?

Mercutio.
The slip, sir, the slip; can you not conceive?

Romeo.
Pardon, good Mercutio, my business was great; and in such a case as mine a man may strain courtesy.

Mercutio.
That's as much as to say, such a case as yours constrains a man to bow in the hams.

Romeo.
Meaning, to court'sy.

Mercutio.
Thou hast most kindly hit it.

Romeo.
A most courteous exposition.

Mercutio.
Nay, I am the very pink of courtesy.

Romeo.
Pink for flower.

Mercutio.
Right.

Romeo.
Why, then is my pump well-flowered.

Mercutio.
Well said: follow me this jest now till thou hast worn out thy pump;that, when the single sole of it is worn, the jest may remain, after the wearing, sole singular.

Romeo.
O single-soled jest, solely singular for the singleness!

Mercutio.
Come between us, good Benvolio; my wits faint.

Romeo.
Swits and spurs, swits and spurs; or I'll cry a match.

Mercutio.
Nay, if thy wits run the wild-goose chase, I have done; for thou hast more of the wild-goose in one of thy wits than, I am sure, I have in my whole five: was I with you there for **the goose?**

Romeo.
Thou wast never with me for anything when thou wast not there for the goose.

Mercutio.
I will bite thee by the ear for that jest.

Romeo.
Nay, good goose, bite not.

Mercutio.
Thy wit is a very bitter sweeting; it is a most sharp sauce.

Romeo.
And is it not, then, well served in to a sweet goose?

Mercutio.
O, here's a wit of cheveril, that stretches from an inch narrow to an ell broad!

Romeo.
I stretch it out for that word broad: which added to the goose, proves thee far and wide a broad goose.

Mercutio.
Why, is not this better now than groaning for love? now art thou sociable, now art thou Romeo; not art thou what thou art, by art as well as by nature: for this drivelling love is like a great natural, that runs lolling up and

down to hide his bauble in a hole.

Benvolio.
Stop there, stop there.

Mercutio.
Thou desirest me to stop in my tale against the hair.

Benvolio.
Thou wouldst else have made thy tale large.

Mercutio.
O, thou art deceived; I would have made it short: for I was come to the whole depth of my tale; and meant indeed to occupy the argument no longer.

Romeo.
Here's goodly gear!

[Enter Nurse and Peter.]

Mercutio.
A sail, a sail, a sail!

Benvolio.
Two, two; a shirt and a smock.

Nurse.
Peter!

Peter.
Anon.

Nurse.
My fan, Peter.

Mercutio.
Good Peter, to hide her face; for her fan's the fairer face.

Nurse.
God ye good morrow, gentlemen.

Mercutio.
God ye good-den, fair gentlewoman.

Nurse.
Is it good-den?

Mercutio.
'Tis no less, I tell ye; for the bawdy hand of the
dial is now upon the prick of noon.

Nurse.
Out upon you! what a man are you!

Romeo.
One, gentlewoman, that God hath made for
himself to mar.

Nurse.
By my troth, it is well said;--for himself to mar,
quoth 'a?--Gentlemen, can any of you tell me
where I may find the young
Romeo?

Romeo.
I can tell you: but young Romeo will be older
when you have found him than he was when you
sought him: I am the youngest of
that name, for fault of a worse.

Nurse.
You say well.

Mercutio.
Yea, is the worst well? very well took, i' faith;
wisely, wisely.

Nurse.
If you be he, sir, I desire some confidence with
you.

Benvolio.
She will indite him to some supper.

Mercutio.
A bawd, a bawd, a bawd! So ho!

Romeo.
What hast thou found?

Mercutio.
No hare, sir; unless a hare, sir, in a lenten pie,
that is
something stale and hoar ere it be spent.
[Sings.]
An old hare hoar,
And an old hare hoar,
Is very good meat in Lent;
But a hare that is hoar
Is too much for a score
When it hoars ere it be spent.

Romeo, will you come to your father's? we'll to
dinner thither.

Romeo.
I will follow you.

Mercutio.
Farewell, ancient lady; farewell,--
[singing] lady, lady, lady.

[Exeunt Mercutio, and Benvolio.]

Nurse.
Marry, farewell!--I pray you, sir, what saucy
merchant was this that was so full of his ropery?

Romeo.
A gentleman, nurse, that loves to hear himself
talk; and will speak more in a minute than he
will stand to in a month.

Nurse.
An 'a speak anything against me, I'll take him
down, an'a were lustier than he is, and twenty
such Jacks; and if I cannot,
I'll find those that shall. Scurvy knave! I am
none of his flirt-gills; I am none of his skains-
mates.--And thou must stand
by too, and suffer every knave to use me at his
pleasure!

Peter. I saw no man use you at his pleasure; if I
had, my weapon should quickly have been out, I
warrant you: I dare draw as
soon as another man, if I see occasion in a good
quarrel, and the law on my side.

Nurse.
Now, afore God, I am so vexed that every part
about me quivers. Scurvy knave!--Pray you, sir,
a word: and, as I told you, my
young lady bid me enquire you out; what she
bade me say I will keep to myself: but first let
me tell ye, if ye should lead
her into a fool's paradise, as they say, it were a
very gross kind of behaviour, as they say: for the
gentlewoman is young;
and, therefore, if you should deal double with
her, truly it were an ill thing to be offered to any
gentlewoman, and very
weak dealing.

Romeo.
Nurse, commend me to thy lady and mistress. I
protest unto thee,--

Nurse.
Good heart, and i' faith I will tell her as much:
Lord,
Lord, she will be a joyful woman.

Romeo.
What wilt thou tell her, nurse? thou dost not
mark me.

Nurse.
I will tell her, sir,--that you do protest: which, as
I take it, is a gentlemanlike offer.

Romeo.
Bid her devise some means to come to shrift
This afternoon;
And there she shall at Friar Lawrence' cell
Be shriv'd and married. Here is for thy pains.

Nurse.
No, truly, sir; not a penny.

Romeo.
Go to; I say you shall.

Nurse.
This afternoon, sir? well, she shall be there.

Romeo.
And stay, good nurse, behind the abbey-wall:
Within this hour my man shall be with thee,
And bring thee cords made like a tackled stair;
Which to the high top-gallant of my joy
Must be my convoy in the secret night.
Farewell; be trusty, and I'll quit thy pains:
Farewell; commend me to thy mistress.

Nurse.
Now God in heaven bless thee!--Hark you, sir.

Romeo.
What say'st thou, my dear nurse?

Nurse.
Is your man secret? Did you ne'er hear say,
Two may keep counsel, putting one away?

Romeo.
I warrant thee, my man's as true as steel.

Nurse.
Well, sir; my mistress is the sweetest lady.--
Lord, Lord! when 'twas a little prating thing,--O,
there's a nobleman in town,
one Paris, that would fain lay knife aboard; but
she, good soul, had as lief see a toad, a very
toad, as see him. I anger
her sometimes, and tell her that Paris is the
properer man; but I'll warrant you, when I say
so, she looks as pale as any
clout in the versal world. Doth not rosemary and
Romeo begin both with a letter?

Romeo.
Ay, nurse; what of that? both with an R.

Nurse.
Ah, mocker! that's the dog's name. R is for the
dog: no; I know it begins with some other letter:-
-and she hath the prettiest
sententious of it, of you and rosemary, that it
would do you good to hear it.

Romeo.
Commend me to thy lady.

Nurse.
Ay, a thousand times. [Exit Romeo.]--Peter!

Peter.
Anon?

Nurse.
Peter, take my fan, and go before.

[Exeunt]

Glossary:

answer it accept it.

captain of compliments in dueling, one who has mastered all the rules and moves.

immortal punning on the moves as both famous and fatal.

passado a forward thrust.

the punto reverso a backhanded thrust.

the hay! term used to indicate that your opponent has been hit.

roe fish eggs.

conceive understand.

bow in the hams make a bow.

I'll cry a match I'll claim the victory.

natural fool; idiot.

bauble a jester's baton with an ornament at the end.

here's goodly gear a large clothes horse, refers to the appearance of the Nurse, who is also described in this scene as a sail. Romeo also continues Mercutio's series of bawdy puns in this scene, as gear refers to the reproductive organs.

ropery roguery.

flirt-gills loose women.

skains-mates cutthroat companions.

tackled stair rope ladder.

quit reward you for.

lay knife aboard lay claim to.

clout any piece of cloth, esp. one for cleaning.

Scene V. Capulet's Garden

Summary:

Juliet is itching to hear news from the Nurse whom she sent to Romeo three hours prior, Juliet awaits impatiently. Knowing Juliet's impatience, the Nurse intentionally teases Juliet by concealing the information of the upcoming wedding. Rather, the Nurse grumbles about her own aches and pains. The Nurse finally concedes the information as Juliet is overcome with anxiety. The Nurse tells Juliet that she is to marry Romeo that afternoon at Friar Laurence's cell. The Nurse then goes to collect the rope ladder for Romeo to climb into Juliet's bedroom that evening.

[Enter Juliet.]

Juliet.
The clock struck nine when I did send the nurse;
In half an hour she promis'd to return.
Perchance she cannot meet him: that's not so.--
O, she is lame! love's heralds should be thoughts,
Which ten times faster glide than the sun's beams,
Driving back shadows over lowering hills:
Therefore do nimble-pinion'd doves draw love,
And therefore hath the wind-swift Cupid wings.
Now is the sun upon the highmost hill
Of this day's journey; and from nine till twelve
Is three long hours,--yet she is not come.
Had she affections and warm youthful blood,

38

She'd be as swift in motion as a ball;
My words would bandy her to my sweet love,
And his to me:
But old folks, many feign as they were dead;
Unwieldy, slow, heavy and pale as lead.--
O God, she comes!
[Enter Nurse and Peter].
O honey nurse, what news?
Hast thou met with him? Send thy man away.

Nurse.
Peter, stay at the gate.

[Exit Peter.]

Juliet.
Now, good sweet nurse,--O Lord, why look'st
thou sad?
Though news be sad, yet tell them merrily;
If good, thou sham'st the music of sweet news
By playing it to me with so sour a face.

Nurse.
I am aweary, give me leave awhile;--
Fie, how my bones ache! what a jaunt have I
had!

Juliet.
I would thou hadst my bones, and I thy news:
Nay, come, I pray thee speak;--good, good
nurse, speak.

Nurse.
Jesu, what haste? can you not stay awhile?
Do you not see that I am out of breath?

Juliet.
How art thou out of breath, when thou hast
breath
To say to me that thou art out of breath?
The excuse that thou dost make in this delay
Is longer than the tale thou dost excuse.
Is thy news good or bad? answer to that;
Say either, and I'll stay the circumstance:
Let me be satisfied, is't good or bad?

Nurse.
Well, you have made a simple choice; you know
not how to choose a man: Romeo! no, not he;
rhough his face be better than any
man's, yet his leg excels all men's; and for a
hand and a foot, and a body,--though they be not
to be talked on, yet they are
past compare: he is not the flower of courtesy,--
but I'll warrant him as gentle as a lamb.--Go thy
ways, wench; serve
God.--What, have you dined at home?

Juliet.
No, no: but all this did I know before.
What says he of our marriage? what of that?

Nurse.
Lord, how my head aches! what a head have I!
It beats as it would fall in twenty pieces.
My back o' t' other side,--O, my back, my back!-
Beshrew your heart for sending me about
To catch my death with jauncing up and down!

Juliet.
I' faith, I am sorry that thou art not well.
Sweet, sweet, sweet nurse, tell me, what says my
love?

Nurse.
Your love says, like an honest gentleman,
And a courteous, and a kind, and a handsome;
And, I warrant, a virtuous,--Where is your
mother?

Juliet.
Where is my mother?--why, she is within;
Where should she be? How oddly thou repliest!
'Your love says, like an honest gentleman,--
'Where is your mother?'

Nurse.
O God's lady dear!
Are you so hot? marry, come up, I trow;
Is this the poultice for my aching bones?
Henceforward, do your messages yourself.

Juliet.
Here's such a coil!--come, what says Romeo?

Nurse.
Have you got leave to go to shrift to-day?

Juliet.
I have.

Nurse.
Then hie you hence to Friar Lawrence' cell;
There stays a husband to make you a wife:
Now comes the wanton blood up in your cheeks,
They'll be in scarlet straight at any news.
Hie you to church; I must another way,
To fetch a ladder, by the which your love
Must climb a bird's nest soon when it is dark:
I am the drudge, and toil in your delight;
But you shall bear the burden soon at night.
Go; I'll to dinner; hie you to the cell.

Juliet.
Hie to high fortune!--honest nurse, farewell.

[Exit]

Glossary:

nimble-pinion'd *swift-winged.*

bandy *to toss or hit back and forth, as a ball.*

feign *to make a false show of; pretend.*

jaunce *trudge up and down.*

coil *commotion; turmoil.*

drudge *a person who does hard, menial, or tedious work.*

Scene VI. *Friar Lawrence's Cell*

Summary:

As Romeo and Friar Laurence await Juliet, the Friar again warns Romeo about the impetuousness of his decision to marry. Romeo agrees, but brazenly counters the most important thing is that he can call her his own, even in the face of possible death. The friar then cautions that sometimes the most desirable pleasures have the most dreadful endings. When Juliet arrives, the Friar takes them both into the church so they can be married.

[Enter Friar Lawrence and Romeo.]

Friar.
So smile the heavens upon this holy act
That after-hours with sorrow chide us not!

Romeo.
Amen, amen! but come what sorrow can,
It cannot countervail the exchange of joy
That one short minute gives me in her sight:
Do thou but close our hands with holy words,
Then love-devouring death do what he dare,--
It is enough I may but call her mine.

Friar.
These violent delights have violent ends,
And in their triumph die; like fire and powder,
Which, as they kiss, consume: the sweetest honey
Is loathsome in his own deliciousness,
And in the taste confounds the appetite:
Therefore love moderately: long love doth so;
Too swift arrives as tardy as too slow.
Here comes the lady:--O, so light a foot
Will ne'er wear out the everlasting flint:
A lover may bestride the gossamer
That idles in the wanton summer air
And yet not fall; so light is vanity.

[Enter Juliet.]

Juliet.
Good-even to my ghostly confessor.

40

Friar.
Romeo shall thank thee, daughter, for us both.

Juliet.
As much to him, else is his thanks too much.

Romeo.
Ah, Juliet, if the measure of thy joy
Be heap'd like mine, and that thy skill be more
To blazon it, then sweeten with thy breath
This neighbour air, and let rich music's tongue
Unfold the imagin'd happiness that both
Receive in either by this dear encounter.

Juliet.
Conceit, more rich in matter than in words,
Brags of his substance, not of ornament:
They are but beggars that can count their worth;
But my true love is grown to such excess,
I cannot sum up sum of half my wealth.

Friar.
Come, come with me, and we will make short
work;
For, by your leaves, you shall not stay alone
Till holy church incorporate two in one.

[Exeunt]

Glossary:

countervail *to match or equal.*

gossamers *filmy cobwebs floating in the air or spread on bushes or grass.*

vanity *earthly pleasures or happiness.*

blazen *declare or celebrate.*

Act III

Scene I. A public Place

Summary:

Benvolio and Mercutio are hanging around on the streets of Verona on a hot day when Tybalt comes looking for Romeo. Benvolio does not want a confrontation with the Capulets but Mercutio intentionally provokes trying to lure Tybalt into a quarrel so that they can fight. When Romeo appears, Tybalt insults him, wanting Romeo to respond to the challenge, but Romeo doesn't because he is now related to Tybalt through his marriage to Juliet. Mercutio, offended by Romeo's unwillingness to fight, responds to Tybalt's insults on Romeo's behalf. Tybalt and Mercutio each draw their swords and fight. Romeo steps between them, trying to stop the fight, but Tybalt stabs Mercutio under Romeo's arm. Mercutio's injury is fatal and he dies crying "A plague o' both your houses!" Enraged over Mercutio's death, Romeo attacks Tybalt and kills him. Romeo has to flee a mob of citizens when the Prince, the heads of the two households, and their wives arrive at the scene. After Benvolio tells what happened, the Prince exiles Romeo from Verona under the penalty of death and orders Lords Montague and Capulet to pay heavy fines.

[Enter Mercutio, Benvolio, Page, and Servants.]

Benvolio.
I pray thee, good Mercutio, let's retire:
The day is hot, the Capulets abroad,
And, if we meet, we shall not scape a brawl;
For now, these hot days, is the mad blood
stirring.

Mercutio.
Thou art like one of these fellows that, when he
enters the confines of a tavern, claps me his
sword upon the table, and says
'God send me no need of thee!' and by the
operation of the second cup draws him on the
drawer, when indeed there is no need.

Benvolio.
Am I like such a fellow?

41

Mercutio.
Come, come, thou art as hot a Jack in thy mood
as any in Italy; and as soon moved to be moody,
and as soon moody to be moved.

Benvolio.
And what to?

Mercutio.
Nay, an there were two such, we should have
none shortly, for one would kill the other. Thou!
why, thou wilt quarrel with a
man that hath a hair more or a hair less in his
beard than thou hast. Thou wilt quarrel with a
man for cracking nuts, having
no other reason but because thou hast hazel
eyes;--what eye but such an eye would spy out
such a quarrel? Thy head is as
full of quarrels as an egg is full of meat; and yet
thy head hath been beaten as addle as an egg for
quarrelling. Thou hast
quarrelled with a man for coughing in the street,
because he hath wakened thy dog that hath lain
asleep in the sun. Didst
thou not fall out with a tailor for wearing his
new doublet before Easter? with another for
tying his new shoes with an old
riband? and yet thou wilt tutor me from
quarrelling!

Benvolio.
An I were so apt to quarrel as thou art, any man
should buy the fee simple of my life for an hour
and a quarter.

Mercutio.
The fee simple! O simple!

Benvolio.
By my head, here come the Capulets.

Mercutio.
By my heel, I care not.

[Enter Tybalt and others.]

Tybalt.
Follow me close, for I will speak to them.--
Gentlemen, good-den: a word with one of you.

Mercutio.
And but one word with one of us? Couple it with
something; make it a word and a blow.

Tybalt.
You shall find me apt enough to that, sir, an you
will give me occasion.

Mercutio.
Could you not take some occasion without
giving?

Tybalt.
Mercutio, thou consortest with Romeo,--

Mercutio.
Consort! what, dost thou make us minstrels? An
thou make minstrels of us, look to hear nothing
but discords: here's my
fiddlestick; here's that shall make you dance.
Zounds, consort!

Benvolio.
We talk here in the public haunt of men:
Either withdraw unto some private place,
And reason coldly of your grievances,
Or else depart; here all eyes gaze on us.

Mercutio.
Men's eyes were made to look, and let them
gaze;
I will not budge for no man's pleasure, I.

Tybalt.
Well, peace be with you, sir.--Here comes my
man.

[Enter Romeo.]

Mercutio.
But I'll be hanged, sir, if he wear your livery:
Marry, go before to field, he'll be your follower;
Your worship in that sense may call him man.

Tybalt.
Romeo, the love I bear thee can afford
No better term than this,--Thou art a villain.

Romeo.
Tybalt, the reason that I have to love thee

Doth much excuse the appertaining rage
To such a greeting. Villain am I none;
Therefore farewell; I see thou know'st me not.

Tybalt.
Boy, this shall not excuse the injuries
That thou hast done me; therefore turn and draw.

Romeo.
I do protest I never injur'd thee;
But love thee better than thou canst devise
Till thou shalt know the reason of my love:
And so good Capulet,--which name I tender
As dearly as mine own,--be satisfied.

Mercutio.
O calm, dishonourable, vile submission!
Alla stoccata carries it away. [Draws.]
Tybalt, you rat-catcher, will you walk?

Tybalt.
What wouldst thou have with me?

Mercutio.
Good king of cats, nothing but one of your nine
lives; that I mean to make bold withal, and, as
you shall use me hereafter,
dry-beat the rest of the eight. Will you pluck
your sword out of his pitcher by the ears? make
haste, lest mine be about your
ears ere it be out.

Tybalt.
I am for you. [Drawing.]

Romeo.
Gentle Mercutio, put thy rapier up.

Mercutio.
Come, sir, your passado.

[They fight.]

Romeo.
Draw, Benvolio; beat down their weapons.--
Gentlemen, for shame! forbear this outrage!--
Tybalt,--Mercutio,--the prince expressly hath
Forbid this bandying in Verona streets.--
Hold, Tybalt!--good Mercutio!--
[Exeunt Tybalt with his Partizans.]

Mercutio.
I am hurt;--
A plague o' both your houses!--I am sped.--
Is he gone, and hath nothing?

Benvolio.
What, art thou hurt?

Mercutio.
Ay, ay, a scratch, a scratch; marry, 'tis enough.--
Where is my page?--go, villain, fetch a surgeon.

[Exit Page.]

Romeo.
Courage, man; the hurt cannot be much.

Mercutio.
No, 'tis not so deep as a well, nor so wide as a
church door; but 'tis enough, 'twill serve: ask for
me to-morrow, and you
shall find me a grave man. I am peppered, I
warrant, for this world.--A plague o' both your
houses!--Zounds, a dog, a rat, a
mouse, a cat, to scratch a man to death! a
braggart, a rogue, a villain, that fights by the
book of arithmetic!--Why the
devil came you between us? I was hurt under
your arm.

Romeo.
I thought all for the best.

Mercutio.
Help me into some house, Benvolio,
Or I shall faint.--A plague o' both your houses!
They have made worms' meat of me:
I have it, and soundly too.--Your houses!

[Exit Mercutio and Benvolio.]

Romeo.
This gentleman, the prince's near ally,
My very friend, hath got his mortal hurt
In my behalf; my reputation stain'd
With Tybalt's slander,--Tybalt, that an hour
Hath been my kinsman.--O sweet Juliet,
Thy beauty hath made me effeminate
And in my temper soften'd valour's steel.

[Re-enter Benvolio.]

Benvolio.
O Romeo, Romeo, brave Mercutio's dead!
That gallant spirit hath aspir'd the clouds,
Which too untimely here did scorn the earth.

Romeo.
This day's black fate on more days doth depend;
This but begins the woe others must end.

Benvolio.
Here comes the furious Tybalt back again.

Romeo.
Alive in triumph! and Mercutio slain!
Away to heaven respective lenity,
And fire-ey'd fury be my conduct now!--

[Re-enter Tybalt.]

Now, Tybalt, take the 'villain' back again
That late thou gavest me; for Mercutio's soul
Is but a little way above our heads,
Staying for thine to keep him company.
Either thou or I, or both, must go with him.

Tybalt.
Thou, wretched boy, that didst consort him here,
Shalt with him hence.

Romeo.
This shall determine that.

[They fight; Tybalt falls.]

Benvolio.
Romeo, away, be gone!
The citizens are up, and Tybalt slain.--
Stand not amaz'd. The prince will doom thee
death
If thou art taken. Hence, be gone, away!

Romeo.
O, I am fortune's fool!

Benvolio.
Why dost thou stay?

[Exit Romeo.]

[Enter Citizens, &c.]

1 Citizen.
Which way ran he that kill'd Mercutio?
Tybalt, that murderer, which way ran he?

Benvolio.
There lies that Tybalt.

1 Citizen.
Up, sir, go with me;
I charge thee in the prince's name obey.

[Enter Prince, attended; Montague, Capulet,
their Wives, and others.]

Prince.
Where are the vile beginners of this fray?

Benvolio.
O noble prince. I can discover all
The unlucky manage of this fatal brawl:
There lies the man, slain by young Romeo,
That slew thy kinsman, brave Mercutio.

Lady Capulet.
Tybalt, my cousin! O my brother's child!--
O prince!--O husband!--O, the blood is spill'd
Of my dear kinsman!--Prince, as thou art true,
For blood of ours shed blood of Montague.--
O cousin, cousin!

Prince.
Benvolio, who began this bloody fray?

Benvolio.
Tybalt, here slain, whom Romeo's hand did slay;
Romeo, that spoke him fair, bid him bethink
How nice the quarrel was, and urg'd withal
Your high displeasure.--All this,--uttered
With gentle breath, calm look, knees humbly
bow'd,--
Could not take truce with the unruly spleen
Of Tybalt, deaf to peace, but that he tilts
With piercing steel at bold Mercutio's breast;
Who, all as hot, turns deadly point to point,
And, with a martial scorn, with one hand beats
Cold death aside, and with the other sends

It back to Tybalt, whose dexterity
Retorts it: Romeo he cries aloud,
'Hold, friends! friends, part!' and swifter than his tongue,
His agile arm beats down their fatal points,
And 'twixt them rushes; underneath whose arm
An envious thrust from Tybalt hit the life
Of stout Mercutio, and then Tybalt fled:
But by-and-by comes back to Romeo,
Who had but newly entertain'd revenge,
And to't they go like lightning; for, ere I
Could draw to part them was stout Tybalt slain;
And as he fell did Romeo turn and fly.
This is the truth, or let Benvolio die.

Lady Capulet.
He is a kinsman to the Montague,
Affection makes him false, he speaks not true:
Some twenty of them fought in this black strife,
And all those twenty could but kill one life.
I beg for justice, which thou, prince, must give;
Romeo slew Tybalt, Romeo must not live.

Prince.
Romeo slew him, he slew Mercutio:
Who now the price of his dear blood doth owe?

Montague.
Not Romeo, prince; he was Mercutio's friend;
His fault concludes but what the law should end,
The life of Tybalt.

Prince.
And for that offence
Immediately we do exile him hence:
I have an interest in your hate's proceeding,
My blood for your rude brawls doth lie a-bleeding;
But I'll amerce you with so strong a fine
That you shall all repent the loss of mine:
I will be deaf to pleading and excuses;
Nor tears nor prayers shall purchase out abuses,
Therefore use none: let Romeo hence in haste,
Else, when he is found, that hour is his last.
Bear hence this body, and attend our will:
Mercy but murders, pardoning those that kill.

[Exeunt]

Glossary:

abroad out and about.

by the operation of the second cup by the time the second cup of liquor has taken effect upon him.

addle muddled and, perhaps, rotten.

doublet a man's close-fitting jacket with or without sleeves, worn chiefly from the 14th to the 16th centuries.

tutor me from quarrelling teach me how to avoid getting into a quarrel.

simple feeble or foolish.

fiddlestick the bow for a fiddle. Mercutio puns on the word as he draws his rapier.

zounds an oath. The abbreviated form of the oath "By God's wounds,"

bandying to give and take; to exchange (words) in an angry or argumentative manner.

sped done for.

ally relative, kinsman.

cousin loosely, any relative by blood or marriage.

aspir'd to rise high; to tower.

conduct guide.

amerce to punish by imposing a fine.

Scene II. A Room in Capulet's House

Summary:

Juliet impatiently awaits nightfall so she can celebrate her wedding night with Romeo. The Nurse arrives and in her sorrow, mistakenly leads Juliet into thinking that Romeo has been killed. When the Nurse finally tells Juliet that it is Tybalt who is dead, Juliet's worries are only somewhat relieved. After hearing Romeo has been banished, Juliet is overcome by grief. The Nurse informs Juliet that Romeo is in hiding at Friar Laurence's cell. Juliet sends the Nurse with a ring, request Romeo to come and "take his last farewell."

[Enter Juliet.]

Juliet.
Gallop apace, you fiery-footed steeds,
Towards Phoebus' lodging; such a waggoner
As Phaeton would whip you to the west
And bring in cloudy night immediately.--
Spread thy close curtain, love-performing night!
That rude eyes may wink, and Romeo
Leap to these arms, untalk'd of and unseen.--
Lovers can see to do their amorous rites
By their own beauties: or, if love be blind,
It best agrees with night.--Come, civil night,
Thou sober-suited matron, all in black,
And learn me how to lose a winning match,
Play'd for a pair of stainless maidenhoods:
Hood my unmann'd blood, bating in my cheeks,
With thy black mantle; till strange love, grown
bold, Think true love acted simple modesty.
Come, night;--come, Romeo;--come, thou day in
night; For thou wilt lie upon the wings of night
Whiter than new snow upon a raven's back.--
Come, gentle night;--come, loving, black-brow'd
night,
Give me my Romeo; and, when he shall die,
Take him and cut him out in little stars,
And he will make the face of heaven so fine
That all the world will be in love with night,
And pay no worship to the garish sun.--
O, I have bought the mansion of a love,
But not possess'd it; and, though I am sold,
Not yet enjoy'd: so tedious is this day
As is the night before some festival
To an impatient child that hath new robes,
And may not wear them. O, here comes my
nurse,
And she brings news; and every tongue that
speaks
But Romeo's name speaks heavenly eloquence.--

[Enter Nurse, with cords.]

Now, nurse, what news? What hast thou there?
the cords
That Romeo bid thee fetch?

Nurse.
Ay, ay, the cords.

[Throws them down.]

Juliet.
Ah me! what news? why dost thou wring thy
hands?

Nurse.
Ah, well-a-day! he's dead, he's dead, he's dead!
We are undone, lady, we are undone!--
Alack the day!--he's gone, he's kill'd, he's dead!

Juliet.
Can heaven be so envious?

Nurse.
Romeo can,
Though heaven cannot.--O Romeo, Romeo!--
Who ever would have thought it?--Romeo!

Juliet.
What devil art thou, that dost torment me thus?
This torture should be roar'd in dismal hell.
Hath Romeo slain himself? say thou but I,
And that bare vowel I shall poison more
Than the death-darting eye of cockatrice:
I am not I if there be such an I;
Or those eyes shut that make thee answer I.
If he be slain, say I; or if not, no:
Brief sounds determine of my weal or woe.

Nurse.
I saw the wound, I saw it with mine eyes,--
God save the mark!--here on his manly breast.
A piteous corse, a bloody piteous corse;
Pale, pale as ashes, all bedaub'd in blood,
All in gore-blood;--I swounded at the sight.

46

Juliet.
O, break, my heart!--poor bankrout, break at once!
To prison, eyes; ne'er look on liberty!
Vile earth, to earth resign; end motion here;
And thou and Romeo press one heavy bier!

Nurse.
O Tybalt, Tybalt, the best friend I had!
O courteous Tybalt! honest gentleman!
That ever I should live to see thee dead!

Juliet.
What storm is this that blows so contrary?
Is Romeo slaughter'd, and is Tybalt dead?
My dear-lov'd cousin, and my dearer lord?--
Then, dreadful trumpet, sound the general doom!
For who is living, if those two are gone?

Nurse.
Tybalt is gone, and Romeo banished;
Romeo that kill'd him, he is banished.

Juliet.
O God!--did Romeo's hand shed Tybalt's blood?

Nurse.
It did, it did; alas the day, it did!

Juliet.
O serpent heart, hid with a flowering face!
Did ever dragon keep so fair a cave?
Beautiful tyrant! fiend angelical!
Dove-feather'd raven! wolvish-ravening lamb!
Despised substance of divinest show!
Just opposite to what thou justly seem'st,
A damned saint, an honourable villain!--
O nature, what hadst thou to do in hell
When thou didst bower the spirit of a fiend
In mortal paradise of such sweet flesh?--
Was ever book containing such vile matter
So fairly bound? O, that deceit should dwell
In such a gorgeous palace!

Nurse.
There's no trust,
No faith, no honesty in men; all perjur'd,
All forsworn, all naught, all dissemblers.--
Ah, where's my man? Give me some aqua vitae.-

These griefs, these woes, these sorrows make me old.
Shame come to Romeo!

Juliet.
Blister'd be thy tongue
For such a wish! he was not born to shame:
Upon his brow shame is asham'd to sit;
For 'tis a throne where honour may be crown'd
Sole monarch of the universal earth.
O, what a beast was I to chide at him!

Nurse.
Will you speak well of him that kill'd your cousin?

Juliet.
Shall I speak ill of him that is my husband?
Ah, poor my lord, what tongue shall smooth thy name,
When I, thy three-hours' wife, have mangled it?-
But wherefore, villain, didst thou kill my cousin?
That villain cousin would have kill'd my husband:
Back, foolish tears, back to your native spring;
Your tributary drops belong to woe,
Which you, mistaking, offer up to joy.
My husband lives, that Tybalt would have slain;
And Tybalt's dead, that would have slain my husband:
All this is comfort; wherefore weep I, then?
Some word there was, worser than Tybalt's death, That murder'd me: I would forget it fain;
But O, it presses to my memory
Like damned guilty deeds to sinners' minds:
'Tybalt is dead, and Romeo banished.'
That 'banished,' that one word 'banished,'
Hath slain ten thousand Tybalts. Tybalt's death
Was woe enough, if it had ended there:
Or, if sour woe delights in fellowship,
And needly will be rank'd with other griefs,--
Why follow'd not, when she said Tybalt's dead,
Thy father, or thy mother, nay, or both,
Which modern lamentation might have mov'd?
But with a rear-ward following Tybalt's death,
'Romeo is banished'--to speak that word
Is father, mother, Tybalt, Romeo, Juliet,
All slain, all dead: 'Romeo is banished,'--
There is no end, no limit, measure, bound,

In that word's death; no words can that woe
sound.— Where is my father and my mother,
nurse?

Nurse.
Weeping and wailing over Tybalt's corse:
Will you go to them? I will bring you thither.

Juliet.
Wash they his wounds with tears: mine shall be
spent,
When theirs are dry, for Romeo's banishment.
Take up those cords. Poor ropes, you are
beguil'd,
Both you and I; for Romeo is exil'd:
He made you for a highway to my bed;
But I, a maid, die maiden-widowed.
Come, cords; come, nurse; I'll to my wedding-
bed;
And death, not Romeo, take my maidenhead!

Nurse.
Hie to your chamber. I'll find Romeo
To comfort you: I wot well where he is.
Hark ye, your Romeo will be here at night:
I'll to him; he is hid at Lawrence' cell.

Juliet.
O, find him! give this ring to my true knight,
And bid him come to take his last farewell.

[Exeunt]

Glossary:

waggoner driver.

As Phaeton . . . immediately Phaeton, the
son of Apollo, was allowed to drive the
chariot of the sun for a day. His reckless
driving nearly set the earth on fire and Zeus,
the king of the gods, struck him dead with a
thunderbolt.

wink close and be unable to see.

civil night sober, serious night.

lose a winning match . . . stainless
maidenhoods that is, win Romeo by
surrendering to him.

unmann'd untrained; also, as yet
husbandless.

cords the rope ladder so that Romeo can
climb up to Juliet's balcony.

death-darting eye of cockatrice a cockatrice
is a fabulous serpent supposedly hatched
from a cock's egg and having power to kill
by a look.

bedaubed smeared or stained with blood.

divinest show excellent appearance.

all naught all wicked.

all dissemblers all liars.

aqua vitae alcoholic spirits.

tributary paying tribute.

modern commonplace.

Scene III. Friar Lawrence's cell

Summary:

*Friar Laurence informs Romeo that the Prince
has sentenced him to exile rather than death.
Romeo is troubled because he views banishment
as a form of living death because he wouldn't be
able to be with Juliet. The Friar attempts to
reason with Romeo, but Romeo is devastated.
The Nurse arrives and conveys to Romeo Juliet's*

anguish. After hearing this, Romeo wants to take his own life but the Nurse stops him. The Friar instructs Romeo to return to Juliet that night as he originally planned, then before dawn, escape to Mantua. The Friar says he will find a way to publicize Romeo and Juliet's marriage and then get a pardon for Romeo to return safely.

[Enter Friar Lawrence.]

Friar.
Romeo, come forth; come forth, thou fearful man.
Affliction is enanmour'd of thy parts,
And thou art wedded to calamity.

[Enter Romeo.]

Romeo.
Father, what news? what is the prince's doom
What sorrow craves acquaintance at my hand,
That I yet know not?

Friar.
Too familiar
Is my dear son with such sour company:
I bring thee tidings of the prince's doom.

Romeo.
What less than doomsday is the prince's doom?

Friar.
A gentler judgment vanish'd from his lips,--
Not body's death, but body's banishment.

Romeo.
Ha, banishment? be merciful, say death;
For exile hath more terror in his look,
Much more than death; do not say banishment.

Friar.
Hence from Verona art thou banished:
Be patient, for the world is broad and wide.

Romeo.
There is no world without Verona walls,
But purgatory, torture, hell itself.
Hence-banished is banish'd from the world,
And world's exile is death,--then banished
Is death mis-term'd: calling death banishment,

Thou cutt'st my head off with a golden axe,
And smil'st upon the stroke that murders me.

Friar.
O deadly sin! O rude unthankfulness!
Thy fault our law calls death; but the kind prince,
Taking thy part, hath brush'd aside the law,
And turn'd that black word death to banishment:
This is dear mercy, and thou see'st it not.

Romeo.
'Tis torture, and not mercy: heaven is here,
Where Juliet lives; and every cat, and dog,
And little mouse, every unworthy thing,
Live here in heaven, and may look on her;
But Romeo may not.--More validity,
More honourable state, more courtship lives
In carrion flies than Romeo: they may seize
On the white wonder of dear Juliet's hand,
And steal immortal blessing from her lips;
Who, even in pure and vestal modesty,
Still blush, as thinking their own kisses sin;
But Romeo may not; he is banished,--
This may flies do, when I from this must fly.
And sayest thou yet that exile is not death!
Hadst thou no poison mix'd, no sharp-ground knife,
No sudden mean of death, though ne'er so mean,
But banished to kill me; banished?
O friar, the damned use that word in hell;
Howlings attend it: how hast thou the heart,
Being a divine, a ghostly confessor,
A sin-absolver, and my friend profess'd,
To mangle me with that word banishment?

Friar.
Thou fond mad man, hear me speak a little,--

Romeo.
O, thou wilt speak again of banishment.

Friar.
I'll give thee armour to keep off that word;
Adversity's sweet milk, philosophy,
To comfort thee, though thou art banished.

Romeo.
Yet banished? Hang up philosophy!
Unless philosophy can make a Juliet,

Displant a town, reverse a prince's doom,
It helps not, it prevails not,--talk no more.

Friar.
O, then I see that madmen have no ears.

Romeo.
How should they, when that wise men have no
eyes?

Friar.
Let me dispute with thee of thy estate.

Romeo.
Thou canst not speak of that thou dost not feel:
Wert thou as young as I, Juliet thy love,
An hour but married, Tybalt murdered,
Doting like me, and like me banished,
Then mightst thou speak, then mightst thou tear
thy hair,
And fall upon the ground, as I do now,
Taking the measure of an unmade grave.

[Knocking within.]

Friar.
Arise; one knocks. Good Romeo, hide thyself.

Romeo.
Not I; unless the breath of heartsick groans,
Mist-like infold me from the search of eyes.

[Knocking.]

Friar.
Hark, how they knock!--Who's there?--Romeo,
arise;
Thou wilt be taken.--Stay awhile;--Stand up;

[Knocking.]

Run to my study.--By-and-by!--God's will!
What simpleness is this.--I come, I come!

[Knocking.]

Who knocks so hard? whence come you? what's
your will?

Nurse.
[Within.] Let me come in, and you shall know
my errand;
I come from Lady Juliet.

Friar.
Welcome then.

[Enter Nurse.]

Nurse.
O holy friar, O, tell me, holy friar,
Where is my lady's lord, where's Romeo?

Friar.
There on the ground, with his own tears made
drunk.

Nurse.
O, he is even in my mistress' case,--
Just in her case!

Friar.
O woeful sympathy!
Piteous predicament!

Nurse.
Even so lies she,
Blubbering and weeping, weeping and
blubbering.--
Stand up, stand up; stand, an you be a man:
For Juliet's sake, for her sake, rise and stand;
Why should you fall into so deep an O?

Romeo.
Nurse!

Nurse.
Ah sir! ah sir!--Well, death's the end of all.

Romeo.
Spakest thou of Juliet? how is it with her?
Doth not she think me an old murderer,
Now I have stain'd the childhood of our joy
With blood remov'd but little from her own?
Where is she? and how doth she/ and what says
My conceal'd lady to our cancell'd love?

Nurse.
O, she says nothing, sir, but weeps and weeps;

And now falls on her bed; and then starts up,
And Tybalt calls; and then on Romeo cries,
And then down falls again.

Romeo.
As if that name,
Shot from the deadly level of a gun,
Did murder her; as that name's cursed hand
Murder'd her kinsman.--O, tell me, friar, tell me,
In what vile part of this anatomy
Doth my name lodge? tell me, that I may sack
The hateful mansion.

[Drawing his sword.]

Friar.
Hold thy desperate hand:
Art thou a man? thy form cries out thou art;
Thy tears are womanish; thy wild acts denote
The unreasonable fury of a beast;
Unseemly woman in a seeming man!
Or ill-beseeming beast in seeming both!
Thou hast amaz'd me: by my holy order,
I thought thy disposition better temper'd.
Hast thou slain Tybalt? wilt thou slay thyself?
And slay thy lady, too, that lives in thee,
By doing damned hate upon thyself?
Why rail'st thou on thy birth, the heaven, and
earth?
Since birth and heaven and earth, all three do
meet
In thee at once; which thou at once wouldst lose.
Fie, fie, thou sham'st thy shape, thy love, thy
wit;
Which, like a usurer, abound'st in all,
And usest none in that true use indeed
Which should bedeck thy shape, thy love, thy
wit:
Thy noble shape is but a form of wax,
Digressing from the valour of a man;
Thy dear love sworn, but hollow perjury,
Killing that love which thou hast vow'd to
cherish;
Thy wit, that ornament to shape and love,
Mis-shapen in the conduct of them both,
Like powder in a skilless soldier's flask,
Is set a-fire by thine own ignorance,
And thou dismember'd with thine own defence.
What, rouse thee, man! thy Juliet is alive,
For whose dear sake thou wast but lately dead;

There art thou happy: Tybalt would kill thee,
But thou slewest Tybalt; there art thou happy
too:
The law, that threaten'd death, becomes thy
friend,
And turns it to exile; there art thou happy:
A pack of blessings lights upon thy back;
Happiness courts thee in her best array;
But, like a misbehav'd and sullen wench,
Thou pout'st upon thy fortune and thy love:--
Take heed, take heed, for such die miserable.
Go, get thee to thy love, as was decreed,
Ascend her chamber, hence and comfort her:
But, look, thou stay not till the watch be set,
For then thou canst not pass to Mantua;
Where thou shalt live till we can find a time
To blaze your marriage, reconcile your friends,
Beg pardon of the prince, and call thee back
With twenty hundred thousand times more joy
Than thou went'st forth in lamentation.--
Go before, nurse: commend me to thy lady;
And bid her hasten all the house to bed,
Which heavy sorrow makes them apt unto.
Romeo is coming.

Nurse.
O Lord, I could have stay'd here all the night
To hear good counsel: O, what learning is!--
My lord, I'll tell my lady you will come.

Romeo.
Do so, and bid my sweet prepare to chide.

Nurse.
Here, sir, a ring she bid me give you, sir:
Hie you, make haste, for it grows very late.

[Exit.]

Romeo.
How well my comfort is reviv'd by this!

Friar.
Go hence; good night! and here stands all your
state:
Either be gone before the watch be set,
Or by the break of day disguis'd from hence.
Sojourn in Mantua; I'll find out your man,
And he shall signify from time to time

Every good hap to you that chances here:
Give me thy hand; 'tis late; farewell; good night.

Romeo.
But that a joy past joy calls out on me,
It were a grief so brief to part with thee:
Farewell.

[Exeunt]

Glossary:

parts attractive qualities.

doom judgment.

world's exile Romeo feels exiled from the world.

validity value or worth.

state rank.

fond foolish.

Displant a town transplant a town; that is, do the near-impossible.

Taking the measure of an unmade grave Romeo is lying on the ground in despair.

simpleness foolishness.

conceal'd lady Juliet, Romeo's secret wife.

cancell'd love Romeo thinks that his killing Tybalt will render his marriage to Juliet null and void.

sack to plunder or loot.

rail'st complain.

usurer . . . usest . . . use indeed alliterative puns on "usury" and "use": Romeo is not putting his talents to their proper use.

form of wax not a real man, no more durable than a wax figure.

pouts upon treats with contempt.

blaze proclaim in public.

sojourn to live somewhere temporarily.

Scene IV. A Room in Capulet's House

Summary:

Late Monday evening, Capulet and Paris talk over how Juliet's heartache over Tybalt's death has kept Paris from continuing his courtship of Juliet. Abruptly, as Paris gets set to leave, Capulet offers Paris Juliet's hand in marriage. He informs Paris that Juliet will submit to his patriarchal wishes and marry Paris on Thursday. Paris enthusiastically agrees to the arrangements, and Lady Capulet is sent to give the news to Juliet.

[Enter Capulet, Lady Capulet, and Paris.]

Capulet.
Things have fallen out, sir, so unluckily
That we have had no time to move our daughter:
Look you, she lov'd her kinsman Tybalt dearly,
And so did I; well, we were born to die.
'Tis very late; she'll not come down to-night:
I promise you, but for your company,
I would have been a-bed an hour ago.

Paris.
These times of woe afford no tune to woo.--
Madam, good night: commend me to your daughter.

Lady Capulet.
I will, and know her mind early to-morrow;
To-night she's mew'd up to her heaviness.

Capulet.
Sir Paris, I will make a desperate tender
Of my child's love: I think she will be rul'd
In all respects by me; nay more, I doubt it not.--
Wife, go you to her ere you go to bed;
Acquaint her here of my son Paris' love;
And bid her, mark you me, on Wednesday next,-
But, soft! what day is this?

Paris.
Monday, my lord.

Capulet.
Monday! ha, ha! Well, Wednesday is too soon,
Thursday let it be;--a Thursday, tell her,
She shall be married to this noble earl.--
Will you be ready? do you like this haste?
We'll keep no great ado,--a friend or two;
For, hark you, Tybalt being slain so late,
It may be thought we held him carelessly,
Being our kinsman, if we revel much:
Therefore we'll have some half a dozen friends,
And there an end. But what say you to
Thursday?

Paris.
My lord, I would that Thursday were to-morrow.

Capulet.
Well, get you gone: o' Thursday be it then.--
Go you to Juliet, ere you go to bed,
Prepare her, wife, against this wedding-day.--
Farewell, my lord.--Light to my chamber, ho!--
Afore me, it is so very very late
That we may call it early by and by.--
Good night.

[Exeunt]

Glossary:

move persaude.

*mew'd up a mew is a cage for molting
hawks. Juliet has shut herself away to
grieve.*

desperate tender bold offer.

*mark you me take notice of what I say; pay
attention.*

soft hush! Wait a moment!

*Ha! ha! Capulet is reflecting on the plans
he is making; he is not laughing.*

ado fuss; trouble; excitement.

*held him carelessly thought little of him,
neglected his memory.*

by and by soon.

Scene V. An open Gallery to Juliet's Chamber, overlooking the Garden.

Summary:

*Romeo and Juliet make their final exchanges of
love Tuesday morning before Romeo leaves for
Mantua. The lovers attempt to avoid the coming
day that will bring their separation by
pretending that it is still night and that the bird
they hear is the nightingale and not the lark, a
morning bird. However, the menacing threat of
the Prince's sentence of death does finally force
the lovers to part.*

*Juliet's mother enters and, thinking that Juliet is
weeping for Tybalt rather than the exile of
Romeo, attempts to comfort Juliet with her plan
to have Romeo poisoned. Lady Capulet then
tries to cheer Juliet up with the joyful news that
she is to marry Paris on Thursday. Juliet is
shocked and informs her mother she cannot get
married so soon.*

*Her father arrives expecting Juliet will be
excited about the wedding he arranged for her.
When she expresses disapproval, he becomes
angry and orders Juliet obey his declaration and
prepare to be married. The Nurse attempts to
defend Juliet but it doesn't work. Capulet makes
a threat to disown his daughter if she continues*

[Enter Romeo and Juliet.]

Juliet.
Wilt thou be gone? it is not yet near day:
It was the nightingale, and not the lark,
That pierc'd the fearful hollow of thine ear;
Nightly she sings on yond pomegranate tree:
Believe me, love, it was the nightingale.

Romeo.
It was the lark, the herald of the morn,
No nightingale: look, love, what envious streaks
Do lace the severing clouds in yonder east:
Night's candles are burnt out, and jocund day
Stands tiptoe on the misty mountain tops.
I must be gone and live, or stay and die.

Juliet.
Yond light is not daylight, I know it, I:
It is some meteor that the sun exhales
To be to thee this night a torch-bearer
And light thee on the way to Mantua:
Therefore stay yet, thou need'st not to be gone.

Romeo.
Let me be ta'en, let me be put to death;
I am content, so thou wilt have it so.
I'll say yon gray is not the morning's eye,
'Tis but the pale reflex of Cynthia's brow;
Nor that is not the lark whose notes do beat
The vaulty heaven so high above our heads:
I have more care to stay than will to go.--
Come, death, and welcome! Juliet wills it so.--
How is't, my soul? let's talk,--it is not day.

Juliet.
It is, it is!--hie hence, be gone, away!
It is the lark that sings so out of tune,
Straining harsh discords and unpleasing sharps.
Some say the lark makes sweet division;
This doth not so, for she divideth us:
Some say the lark and loathed toad change eyes;
O, now I would they had chang'd voices too!
Since arm from arm that voice doth us affray,

Hunting thee hence with hunt's-up to the day.
O, now be gone; more light and light it grows.

Romeo.
More light and light,--more dark and dark our woes!

[Enter Nurse.]

Nurse.
Madam!

Juliet.
Nurse?

Nurse.
Your lady mother is coming to your chamber:
The day is broke; be wary, look about.

[Exit.]

Juliet.
Then, window, let day in, and let life out.

Romeo.
Farewell, farewell! one kiss, and I'll descend.

[Descends.]

Juliet.
Art thou gone so? my lord, my love, my friend!
I must hear from thee every day i' the hour,
For in a minute there are many days:
O, by this count I shall be much in years
Ere I again behold my Romeo!

Romeo.
Farewell!
I will omit no opportunity
That may convey my greetings, love, to thee.

Juliet.
O, think'st thou we shall ever meet again?

Romeo.
I doubt it not; and all these woes shall serve
For sweet discourses in our time to come.

Juliet.
O God! I have an ill-divining soul!
Methinks I see thee, now thou art below,
As one dead in the bottom of a tomb:
Either my eyesight fails, or thou look'st pale.

Romeo.
And trust me, love, in my eye so do you:
Dry sorrow drinks our blood. Adieu, adieu!

[Exit below.]

Juliet.
O fortune, fortune! all men call thee fickle:
If thou art fickle, what dost thou with him
That is renown'd for faith? Be fickle, fortune;
For then, I hope, thou wilt not keep him long
But send him back.

Lady Capulet.
[Within.] Ho, daughter! are you up?

Juliet.
Who is't that calls? is it my lady mother?
Is she not down so late, or up so early?
What unaccustom'd cause procures her hither?

[Enter Lady Capulet.]

Lady Capulet.
Why, how now, Juliet?

Juliet.
Madam, I am not well.

Lady Capulet.
Evermore weeping for your cousin's death?
What, wilt thou wash him from his grave with
tears?
An if thou couldst, thou couldst not make him
live;
Therefore have done: some grief shows much of
love;
But much of grief shows still some want of wit.

Juliet.
Yet let me weep for such a feeling loss.

Lady Capulet.
So shall you feel the loss, but not the friend
Which you weep for.

Juliet.
Feeling so the loss,
I cannot choose but ever weep the friend.

Lady Capulet.
Well, girl, thou weep'st not so much for his
death
As that the villain lives which slaughter'd him.

Juliet.
What villain, madam?

Lady Capulet.
That same villain Romeo.

Juliet.
Villain and he be many miles asunder.--
God pardon him! I do, with all my heart;
And yet no man like he doth grieve my heart.

Lady Capulet.
That is because the traitor murderer lives.

Juliet.
Ay, madam, from the reach of these my hands.
Would none but I might venge my cousin's
death!

Lady Capulet.
We will have vengeance for it, fear thou not:
Then weep no more. I'll send to one in Mantua,--
Where that same banish'd runagate doth live,
Shall give him such an unaccustom'd dram
That he shall soon keep Tybalt company:
And then I hope thou wilt be satisfied.

Juliet.
Indeed I never shall be satisfied
With Romeo till I behold him--dead--
Is my poor heart so for a kinsman vex'd:
Madam, if you could find out but a man
To bear a poison, I would temper it,
That Romeo should, upon receipt thereof,
Soon sleep in quiet. O, how my heart abhors
To hear him nam'd,--and cannot come to him,--

To wreak the love I bore my cousin Tybalt
Upon his body that hath slaughter'd him!

Lady Capulet.
Find thou the means, and I'll find such a man.
But now I'll tell thee joyful tidings, girl.

Juliet.
And joy comes well in such a needy time:
What are they, I beseech your ladyship?

Lady Capulet.
Well, well, thou hast a careful father, child;
One who, to put thee from thy heaviness,
Hath sorted out a sudden day of joy
That thou expect'st not, nor I look'd not for.

Juliet.
Madam, in happy time, what day is that?

Lady Capulet.
Marry, my child, early next Thursday morn
The gallant, young, and noble gentleman,
The County Paris, at St. Peter's Church,
Shall happily make thee there a joyful bride.

Juliet.
Now by Saint Peter's Church, and Peter too,
He shall not make me there a joyful bride.
I wonder at this haste; that I must wed
Ere he that should be husband comes to woo.
I pray you, tell my lord and father, madam,
I will not marry yet; and when I do, I swear
It shall be Romeo, whom you know I hate,
Rather than Paris:--these are news indeed!

Lady Capulet.
Here comes your father: tell him so yourself,
And see how he will take it at your hands.

[Enter Capulet and Nurse.]

Capulet.
When the sun sets, the air doth drizzle dew;
But for the sunset of my brother's son
It rains downright.--
How now! a conduit, girl? what, still in tears?
Evermore showering? In one little body
Thou counterfeit'st a bark, a sea, a wind:
For still thy eyes, which I may call the sea,

Do ebb and flow with tears; the bark thy body is,
Sailing in this salt flood; the winds, thy sighs;
Who,--raging with thy tears and they with them,--
Without a sudden calm, will overset
Thy tempest-tossed body.--How now, wife!
Have you deliver'd to her our decree?

Lady Capulet.
Ay, sir; but she will none, she gives you thanks.
I would the fool were married to her grave!

Capulet.
Soft! take me with you, take me with you, wife.
How! will she none? doth she not give us thanks?
Is she not proud? doth she not count her bles'd,
Unworthy as she is, that we have wrought
So worthy a gentleman to be her bridegroom?

Juliet.
Not proud you have; but thankful that you have:
Proud can I never be of what I hate;
But thankful even for hate that is meant love.

Capulet.
How now, how now, chop-logic! What is this?
Proud,--and, I thank you,--and I thank you not;--
And yet not proud:--mistress minion, you,
Thank me no thankings, nor proud me no prouds,
But fettle your fine joints 'gainst Thursday next
To go with Paris to Saint Peter's Church,
Or I will drag thee on a hurdle thither.
Out, you green-sickness carrion! out, you baggage!
You tallow-face!

Lady Capulet.
Fie, fie! what, are you mad?

Juliet.
Good father, I beseech you on my knees,
Hear me with patience but to speak a word.

Capulet.
Hang thee, young baggage! disobedient wretch!
I tell thee what,--get thee to church o' Thursday,
Or never after look me in the face:
Speak not, reply not, do not answer me;

My fingers itch.--Wife, we scarce thought us bles'd
That God had lent us but this only child;
But now I see this one is one too much,
And that we have a curse in having her:
Out on her, hilding!

Nurse.
God in heaven bless her!--
You are to blame, my lord, to rate her so.

Capulet.
And why, my lady wisdom? hold your tongue,
Good prudence; smatter with your gossips, go.

Nurse.
I speak no treason.

Capulet.
O, God ye good-en!

Nurse.
May not one speak?

Capulet.
Peace, you mumbling fool!
Utter your gravity o'er a gossip's bowl,
For here we need it not.

Lady Capulet.
You are too hot.

Capulet.
God's bread! it makes me mad:
Day, night, hour, time, tide, work, play,
Alone, in company, still my care hath been
To have her match'd, and having now provided
A gentleman of noble parentage,
Of fair demesnes, youthful, and nobly train'd,
Stuff'd, as they say, with honourable parts,
Proportion'd as one's heart would wish a man,--
And then to have a wretched puling fool,
A whining mammet, in her fortune's tender,
To answer, 'I'll not wed,--I cannot love,
I am too young,--I pray you pardon me:'--
But, an you will not wed, I'll pardon you:
Graze where you will, you shall not house with me:
Look to't, think on't, I do not use to jest.
Thursday is near; lay hand on heart, advise:

An you be mine, I'll give you to my friend;
An you be not, hang, beg, starve, die i' the streets,
For, by my soul, I'll ne'er acknowledge thee,
Nor what is mine shall never do thee good:
Trust to't, bethink you, I'll not be forsworn.

[Exit.]

Juliet.
Is there no pity sitting in the clouds,
That sees into the bottom of my grief?
O, sweet my mother, cast me not away!
Delay this marriage for a month, a week;
Or, if you do not, make the bridal bed
In that dim monument where Tybalt lies.

Lady Capulet.
Talk not to me, for I'll not speak a word;
Do as thou wilt, for I have done with thee.

[Exit.]

Juliet.
O God!--O nurse! how shall this be prevented?
My husband is on earth, my faith in heaven;
How shall that faith return again to earth,
Unless that husband send it me from heaven
By leaving earth?--comfort me, counsel me.--
Alack, alack, that heaven should practise stratagems
Upon so soft a subject as myself!--
What say'st thou? hast thou not a word of joy?
Some comfort, nurse.

Nurse.
Faith, here 'tis; Romeo
Is banished; and all the world to nothing
That he dares ne'er come back to challenge you;
Or if he do, it needs must be by stealth.
Then, since the case so stands as now it doth,
I think it best you married with the county.
O, he's a lovely gentleman!
Romeo's a dishclout to him; an eagle, madam,
Hath not so green, so quick, so fair an eye
As Paris hath. Beshrew my very heart,
I think you are happy in this second match,
For it excels your first: or if it did not,
Your first is dead; or 'twere as good he were,
As living here, and you no use of him.

Juliet.
Speakest thou this from thy heart?

Nurse.
And from my soul too;
Or else beshrew them both.

Juliet.
Amen!

Nurse.
What?

Juliet.
Well, thou hast comforted me marvellous much.
Go in; and tell my lady I am gone,
Having displeas'd my father, to Lawrence' cell,
To make confession and to be absolv'd.

Nurse.
Marry, I will; and this is wisely done.

[Exit.]

Juliet.
Ancient damnation! O most wicked fiend!
Is it more sin to wish me thus forsworn,
Or to dispraise my lord with that same tongue
Which she hath prais'd him with above compare
So many thousand times?--Go, counsellor;
Thou and my bosom henceforth shall be twain.--
I'll to the friar to know his remedy;
If all else fail, myself have power to die.

[Exeunt]

Glossary:

night's candles the stars.

Cynthia's brow the moon.

care desire.

hunt's-up morning song used to wake
huntsmen and, more traditionally, a newly
married bride.

runagate fugitive (runaway).

dram potion.

wrought arranged for.

mistress minion spoiled hussy.

hurdle a kind of frame or sled on which
prisoners in England were drawn through
the streets to execution.

hilding a low, contemptible person.

rate to scold severely; chide.

smatter to utter or gossip; an onomatopoeic
word like "chatter."

demesnes the land around a mansion; lands
of an estate.

puling fool whimpering child.

mammet doll or puppet.

challenge claim.

dishclout a cloth for washing dishes.

beshrew to curse: mainly in mild
imprecations.

Act IV

Scene I. Friar Lawrence's Cell

Summary:

*Tuesday morning Paris informs Friar Laurence
of his planned marriage to Juliet — a wedding
scheduled to take place in two days. The Friar*

expresses worry that the wedding has been prepared too quickly, and he gives various reasons to delay the ceremony. Paris thinks that Capulet rushed the wedding out of concern for Juliet's sorrow over the death of Tybalt..

Juliet gets to the Friar's cell and succeeds in cleverly avoiding Paris' compliments and the references he makes to their upcoming marriage. After Paris leaves, Juliet begs the Friar for an answer to her tragic predicament fearing death is her only option. The Friar gives Juliet a solution — a sleeping potion that she is can take on Wednesday night, the evening before the wedding. The potion will cause Juliet to fall unconscious, making her appear dead for 42 hours. During that time, her body will rest in the family tomb. The Friar affirms he will let Romeo know of this plan. Juliet promptly agrees and departs with the potion.

[Enter Friar Lawrence and Paris.]

Friar.
On Thursday, sir? the time is very short.

Paris.
My father Capulet will have it so;
And I am nothing slow to slack his haste.

Friar.
You say you do not know the lady's mind:
Uneven is the course; I like it not.

Parls.
Immoderately she weeps for Tybalt's death,
And therefore have I little talk'd of love;
For Venus smiles not in a house of tears.
Now, sir, her father counts it dangerous
That she do give her sorrow so much sway;
And, in his wisdom, hastes our marriage,
To stop the inundation of her tears;
Which, too much minded by herself alone,
May be put from her by society:
Now do you know the reason of this haste.

Friar.
[Aside.] I would I knew not why it should be slow'd.--
Look, sir, here comes the lady toward my cell.

[Enter Juliet.]

Paris.
Happily met, my lady and my wife!

Juliet.
That may be, sir, when I may be a wife.

Paris.
That may be must be, love, on Thursday next.

Juliet.
What must be shall be.

Friar.
That's a certain text.

Paris.
Come you to make confession to this father?

Juliet.
To answer that, I should confess to you.

Paris.
Do not deny to him that you love me.

Juliet.
I will confess to you that I love him.

Paris.
So will ye, I am sure, that you love me.

Juliet.
If I do so, it will be of more price,
Being spoke behind your back than to your face.

Paris.
Poor soul, thy face is much abus'd with tears.

Juliet.
The tears have got small victory by that;
For it was bad enough before their spite.

Paris.
Thou wrong'st it more than tears with that report.

Juliet.

That is no slander, sir, which is a truth;
And what I spake, I spake it to my face.

Paris.
Thy face is mine, and thou hast slander'd it.

Juliet.
It may be so, for it is not mine own.--
Are you at leisure, holy father, now;
Or shall I come to you at evening mass?

Friar.
My leisure serves me, pensive daughter, now.--
My lord, we must entreat the time alone.

Paris.
God shield I should disturb devotion!--
Juliet, on Thursday early will I rouse you:
Till then, adieu; and keep this holy kiss.

[Exit.]

Juliet.
O, shut the door! and when thou hast done so,
Come weep with me; past hope, past cure, past
help!

Friar.
Ah, Juliet, I already know thy grief;
It strains me past the compass of my wits:
I hear thou must, and nothing may prorogue it,
On Thursday next be married to this county.

Juliet.
Tell me not, friar, that thou hear'st of this,
Unless thou tell me how I may prevent it:
If, in thy wisdom, thou canst give no help,
Do thou but call my resolution wise,
And with this knife I'll help it presently.
God join'd my heart and Romeo's, thou our
hands;
And ere this hand, by thee to Romeo's seal'd,
Shall be the label to another deed,
Or my true heart with treacherous revolt
Turn to another, this shall slay them both:
Therefore, out of thy long-experienc'd time,
Give me some present counsel; or, behold,
'Twixt my extremes and me this bloody knife
Shall play the empire; arbitrating that
Which the commission of thy years and art

Could to no issue of true honour bring.
Be not so long to speak; I long to die,
If what thou speak'st speak not of remedy.

Friar.
Hold, daughter. I do spy a kind of hope,
Which craves as desperate an execution
As that is desperate which we would prevent.
If, rather than to marry County Paris
Thou hast the strength of will to slay thyself,
Then is it likely thou wilt undertake
A thing like death to chide away this shame,
That cop'st with death himself to scape from it;
And, if thou dar'st, I'll give thee remedy.

Juliet.
O, bid me leap, rather than marry Paris,
From off the battlements of yonder tower;
Or walk in thievish ways; or bid me lurk
Where serpents are; chain me with roaring bears;
Or shut me nightly in a charnel-house,
O'er-cover'd quite with dead men's rattling
bones,
With reeky shanks and yellow chapless skulls;
Or bid me go into a new-made grave,
And hide me with a dead man in his shroud;
Things that, to hear them told, have made me
tremble;
And I will do it without fear or doubt,
To live an unstain'd wife to my sweet love.

Friar.
Hold, then; go home, be merry, give consent
To marry Paris: Wednesday is to-morrow;
To-morrow night look that thou lie alone,
Let not thy nurse lie with thee in thy chamber:
Take thou this vial, being then in bed,
And this distilled liquor drink thou off:
When, presently, through all thy veins shall run
A cold and drowsy humour; for no pulse
Shall keep his native progress, but surcease:
No warmth, no breath, shall testify thou livest;
The roses in thy lips and cheeks shall fade
To paly ashes; thy eyes' windows fall,
Like death, when he shuts up the day of life;
Each part, depriv'd of supple government,
Shall, stiff and stark and cold, appear like death:
And in this borrow'd likeness of shrunk death
Thou shalt continue two-and-forty hours,
And then awake as from a pleasant sleep.

Now, when the bridegroom in the morning comes
To rouse thee from thy bed, there art thou dead:
Then,--as the manner of our country is,--
In thy best robes, uncover'd, on the bier,
Thou shalt be borne to that same ancient vault
Where all the kindred of the Capulets lie.
In the mean time, against thou shalt awake,
Shall Romeo by my letters know our drift;
And hither shall he come: and he and I
Will watch thy waking, and that very night
Shall Romeo bear thee hence to Mantua.
And this shall free thee from this present shame,
If no inconstant toy nor womanish fear
Abate thy valour in the acting it.

Juliet.
Give me, give me! O, tell not me of fear!

Friar.
Hold; get you gone, be strong and prosperous
In this resolve: I'll send a friar with speed
To Mantua, with my letters to thy lord.

Juliet.
Love give me strength! and strength shall help afford.
Farewell, dear father.

[Exeunt]

Glossary:

nothing slow to slack his haste *by no means reluctant if I should slow him down in his haste.*

uneven is the course *the decision is arbitrary and one-sided.*

society *companionship.*

pensive *sad; melancholy.*

shield *forbid.*

prorogue *postpone; delay.*

extremes *severe difficulties.*

cop'st *is willing to face or encounter.*

charnel house *a building or place where corpses or bones are deposited.*

reeky *emitting a strong, unpleasant smell.*

chapless *without the lower jaw.*

humour *fluid.*

surcease *cease; stop.*

wanny *pale.*

supple government *muscular movement.*

stark *stiff or rigid, as a corpse.*

drift *intention.*

toy *triviality.*

Scene II. Hall in Capulet's House

Summary:

Juliet gets back to the Capulet house and sees wedding preparations are well underway. She informs her father that she will conform to his wishes and agree to marry Paris. Lord Capulet is so ecstatic of the news that he decides to move the wedding from Thursday to Wednesday. Lady Capulet objects, stating that such quick notice will not allow enough time to prepare. The elated Lord Capulet ignores her. Juliet is now scheduled to get married the following morning.

[Enter Capulet, Lady Capulet, Nurse, and Servants.]

Capulet.
So many guests invite as here are writ.--

[Exit first Servant.]

Sirrah, go hire me twenty cunning cooks.

2 Servant.
You shall have none ill, sir; for I'll try if they can
lick their fingers.

Capulet.
How canst thou try them so?

2 Servant.
Marry, sir, 'tis an ill cook that cannot lick his
own fingers:
therefore he that cannot lick his fingers goes not
with me.

Capulet.
Go, begone.--

[Exit second Servant.]

We shall be much unfurnish'd for this time.--
What, is my daughter gone to Friar Lawrence?

Nurse.
Ay, forsooth.

Capulet.
Well, be may chance to do some good on her:
A peevish self-will'd harlotry it is.

Nurse.
See where she comes from shrift with merry
look.

[Enter Juliet.]

Capulet.
How now, my headstrong! where have you been
gadding?

Juliet.
Where I have learn'd me to repent the sin
Of disobedient opposition
To you and your behests; and am enjoin'd
By holy Lawrence to fall prostrate here,
To beg your pardon:--pardon, I beseech you!
Henceforward I am ever rul'd by you.

Capulet.
Send for the county; go tell him of this:
I'll have this knot knit up to-morrow morning.

Juliet.
I met the youthful lord at Lawrence' cell;
And gave him what becomed love I might,
Not stepping o'er the bounds of modesty.

Capulet.
Why, I am glad on't; this is well,--stand up,--
This is as't should be.--Let me see the county;
Ay, marry, go, I say, and fetch him hither.--
Now, afore God, this reverend holy friar,
All our whole city is much bound to him.

Juliet.
Nurse, will you go with me into my closet,
To help me sort such needful ornaments
As you think fit to furnish me to-morrow?

Lady Capulet.
No, not till Thursday; there is time enough.

Capulet.
Go, nurse, go with her.--We'll to church to-
morrow.

[Exeunt Juliet and Nurse.]

Lady Capulet.
We shall be short in our provision:
'Tis now near night.

Capulet.
Tush, I will stir about,
And all things shall be well, I warrant thee, wife:
Go thou to Juliet, help to deck up her;
I'll not to bed to-night;--let me alone;
I'll play the housewife for this once.--What, ho!-
They are all forth: well, I will walk myself
To County Paris, to prepare him up
Against to-morrow: my heart is wondrous light
Since this same wayward girl is so reclaim'd.

[Exeunt]

Glossary:

none ill *no bad ones.*

62

I'll try . . . fingers from the saying that only bad cooks will not be able to lick their own fingers; that is, the servants will see if they are willing to test their own cooking.

unfurnish'd unprepared, without supplies.

forsooth yes indeed.

harlotry willful behavior or hussy. Capulet regards his daughter with contempt.

gadding wandering about in an idle or restless way.

enjoined ordered.

becomed befitting; becoming.

bound obliged or indebted.

closet a small room or cupboard for clothes.

provision food and other supplies.

Scene III. Juliet's Chamber

Summary:

Juliet and her nurse make final preparations for the wedding that is scheduled to take place the next morning. Lady Capulet offers to help, but Juliet requests to be left to her prayer. She sends the Nurse and her mother away and thinks about the Friar's scheme. She speculates on whether the Friar gave her actual poison to cover his part in marrying a Capulet and a Montague. She decides she has to trust the Friar and if the potion doesn't work, she will choose to die rather than marry Paris. She places a dagger by her bedside just in case. Juliet's imagination takes off as she envisions the tragedy she will face if the plan does not work and she awakens in the tomb alone. After Juliet imagines Tybalt's ghost going toward Romeo for revenge she gets enough nerve to take the potion and intercept Tybalt:

*O look, methinks I see my cousin's ghost
Seeking out Romeo that did spit his body
Upon a rapier's point! Stay, Tybalt, stay!*

[Enter Juliet and Nurse.]

Juliet.
Ay, those attires are best:--but, gentle nurse,
I pray thee, leave me to myself to-night;
For I have need of many orisons
To move the heavens to smile upon my state,
Which, well thou know'st, is cross and full of sin.

[Enter Lady Capulet.]

Lady Capulet.
What, are you busy, ho? need you my help?

Juliet.
No, madam; we have cull'd such necessaries
As are behoveful for our state to-morrow:
So please you, let me now be left alone,
And let the nurse this night sit up with you;
For I am sure you have your hands full all
In this so sudden business.

Lady Capulet.
Good night:
Get thee to bed, and rest; for thou hast need.

[Exeunt Lady Capulet and Nurse.]

Juliet.
Farewell!--God knows when we shall meet again.
I have a faint cold fear thrills through my veins
That almost freezes up the heat of life:
I'll call them back again to comfort me;--
Nurse!--What should she do here?
My dismal scene I needs must act alone.--
Come, vial.--
What if this mixture do not work at all?
Shall I be married, then, to-morrow morning?--
No, No!--this shall forbid it:--lie thou there.--

[Laying down her dagger.]

What if it be a poison, which the friar
Subtly hath minister'd to have me dead,

63

Lest in this marriage he should be dishonour'd,
Because he married me before to Romeo?
I fear it is: and yet methinks it should not,
For he hath still been tried a holy man:--
I will not entertain so bad a thought.--
How if, when I am laid into the tomb,
I wake before the time that Romeo
Come to redeem me? there's a fearful point!
Shall I not then be stifled in the vault,
To whose foul mouth no healthsome air breathes in,
And there die strangled ere my Romeo comes?
Or, if I live, is it not very like
The horrible conceit of death and night,
Together with the terror of the place,--
As in a vault, an ancient receptacle,
Where, for this many hundred years, the bones
Of all my buried ancestors are pack'd;
Where bloody Tybalt, yet but green in earth,
Lies festering in his shroud; where, as they say,
At some hours in the night spirits resort;--
Alack, alack, is it not like that I,
So early waking,--what with loathsome smells,
And shrieks like mandrakes torn out of the earth,
That living mortals, hearing them, run mad;--
O, if I wake, shall I not be distraught,
Environed with all these hideous fears?
And madly play with my forefathers' joints?
And pluck the mangled Tybalt from his shroud?
And, in this rage, with some great kinsman's bone,
As with a club, dash out my desperate brains?--
O, look! methinks I see my cousin's ghost
Seeking out Romeo, that did spit his body
Upon a rapier's point:--stay, Tybalt, stay!--
Romeo, I come! this do I drink to thee.

[Throws herself on the bed.]

Glossary:

orisons prayers.

state circumstances.

cross unfavorable.

culled picked out; selected.

behoveful necessary or required.

faint cold fear fear causing a chilling faintness.

subtly hath ministered cunningly has administered.

tried proved.

conceit thought.

receptacle repository or sepulcher.

shrieks like mandrakes a mandrake is a poisonous plant whose root was thought to have magic powers because of its fancied resemblance to the human body. It was believed that the mandrake would shriek as it was pulled out of the ground, and to hear a mandrake's shriek was thought to bring death or madness.

environ'd with surrounded by.

rage insanity, madness.

Scene IV. Hall in Capulet's House

Summary:

It's 3 a.m., and Lord Capulet is still up. The Capulet household has been busy throughout the night with frantic wedding preparations being made. As sunrise approaches, Capulet hears music indicating Paris is nearing the house. He orders the Nurse to wake up Juliet.

[Enter Lady Capulet and Nurse.]

Lady Capulet.
Hold, take these keys and fetch more spices, nurse.

Nurse.
They call for dates and quinces in the pastry.

[Enter Capulet.]

Capulet.
Come, stir, stir, stir! The second cock hath

crow'd,
The curfew bell hath rung, 'tis three o'clock:--
Look to the bak'd meats, good Angelica;
Spare not for cost.

Nurse.
Go, you cot-quean, go,
Get you to bed; faith, you'll be sick to-morrow
For this night's watching.

Capulet.
No, not a whit: what! I have watch'd ere now
All night for lesser cause, and ne'er been sick.

Lady Capulet.
Ay, you have been a mouse-hunt in your time;
But I will watch you from such watching now.

[Exeunt Lady Capulet and Nurse.]

Capulet.
A jealous-hood, a jealous-hood!--Now, fellow,

[Enter Servants, with spits, logs and baskets.]

What's there?

1 Servant.
Things for the cook, sir; but I know not what.

Capulet.
Make haste, make haste. [Exit 1 Servant.]
--Sirrah, fetch drier logs:
Call Peter, he will show thee where they are.

2 Servant.
I have a head, sir, that will find out logs
And never trouble Peter for the matter.

[Exit.]

Capulet.
Mass, and well said; a merry whoreson, ha!
Thou shalt be logger-head.--Good faith, 'tis day.
The county will be here with music straight,
For so he said he would:--I hear him near.
[Music within.]
Nurse!--wife!--what, ho!--what, nurse, I say!

[Re-enter Nurse.]

Go, waken Juliet; go and trim her up;
I'll go and chat with Paris:--hie, make haste,
Make haste; the bridegroom he is come already:
Make haste, I say.

[Exeunt.]

Glossary:

pastry *place where pastry is made.*

curfew bell *the bell used especially in the medieval and renaissance periods, which rang in the morning and evening to signal curfew.*

cot-quean *a man who usurped the place of the housewife. The Nurse teases Capulet for the pride and concern he takes in household affairs.*

lesser cause *that is, a woman, an amorous liaison.*

you have been a mouse-hunt in your time *you have chased after women in your youth. "Mouse" was an amorous term for a woman and here suggests the image of a cat prowling after a mouse.*

jealous hood *jealous wife. Capulet is humorously responding to his wife's remarks about his past.*

loggerhead *a stupid fellow; blockhead. Capulet puns on the second servant's ability to find logs for the fire.*

Scene V. Juliet's Chamber; Juliet on the bed

Summary

The scene opens on Wednesday morning. The Nurse enters Juliet's quarters and discovers her unresponsive body on the bed. The Nurse attempts to wake her, but thinking she is dead, cries out to the family in panic. The Capulets,

Friar Laurence, and Paris enter the room in reaction to the Nurse's cries. They intensely grieve Juliet's loss as the Friar maintains his trickery by giving words of comfort regarding Divine Will, consoling the family by conveying the belief that Juliet is in heaven. The Friar arranges for Juliet's body to be taken to the family vault. Capulet pronounces that the wedding arrangements be changed to funeral preparations. The scene concludes with a witty interlude between the wedding musicians and Peter, a Capulet servant, as they participate in indecent banter.

[Enter Nurse.]

Nurse.
Mistress!--what, mistress!--Juliet!--fast, I
warrant her, she:--
Why, lamb!--why, lady!--fie, you slug-abed!--
Why, love, I say!--madam! sweetheart!--why,
bride!--
What, not a word?--you take your pennyworths
now;
Sleep for a week; for the next night, I warrant,
The County Paris hath set up his rest
That you shall rest but little.--God forgive me!
Marry, and amen, how sound is she asleep!
I needs must wake her.--Madam, madam,
madam!--
Ay, let the county take you in your bed;
He'll fright you up, i' faith.--Will it not be?
What, dress'd! and in your clothes! and down
again!
I must needs wake you.--lady! lady! lady!--
Alas, alas!--Help, help! My lady's dead!--
O, well-a-day that ever I was born!--
Some aqua-vitae, ho!--my lord! my lady!

[Enter Lady Capulet.]

Lady Capulet
What noise is here?

Nurse.
O lamentable day!

Lady Capulet.
What is the matter?

Nurse.
Look, look! O heavy day!

Lady Capulet.
O me, O me!--my child, my only life!
Revive, look up, or I will die with thee!--
Help, help!--call help.

[Enter Capulet.]

Capulet.
For shame, bring Juliet forth; her lord is come.

Nurse.
She's dead, deceas'd, she's dead; alack the day!

Lady Capulet
Alack the day, she's dead, she's dead, she's dead!

Capulet.
Ha! let me see her:--out alas! she's cold;
Her blood is settled, and her joints are stiff;
Life and these lips have long been separated:
Death lies on her like an untimely frost
Upon the sweetest flower of all the field.
Accursed time! unfortunate old man!

Nurse.
O lamentable day!

Lady Capulet.
O woful time!

Capulet.
Death, that hath ta'en her hence to make me
wail,
Ties up my tongue and will not let me speak.

[Enter Friar Lawrence and Paris, with
Musicians.]

Friar.
Come, is the bride ready to go to church?

Capulet.
Ready to go, but never to return:--
O son, the night before thy wedding day
Hath death lain with thy bride:--there she lies,
Flower as she was, deflowered by him.

Death is my son-in-law, death is my heir;
My daughter he hath wedded: I will die.
And leave him all; life, living, all is death's.

Paris.
Have I thought long to see this morning's face,
And doth it give me such a sight as this?

Lady Capulet.
Accurs'd, unhappy, wretched, hateful day!
Most miserable hour that e'er time saw
In lasting labour of his pilgrimage!
But one, poor one, one poor and loving child,
But one thing to rejoice and solace in,
And cruel death hath catch'd it from my sight!

Nurse.
O woe! O woeful, woeful, woeful day!
Most lamentable day, most woeful day
That ever, ever, I did yet behold!
O day! O day! O day! O hateful day!
Never was seen so black a day as this:
O woeful day! O woeful day!

Paris.
Beguil'd, divorced, wronged, spited, slain!
Most detestable death, by thee beguil'd,
By cruel cruel thee quite overthrown!--
O love! O life!--not life, but love in death!

Capulet.
Despis'd, distressed, hated, martyr'd, kill'd!--
Uncomfortable time, why cam'st thou now
To murder, murder our solemnity?--
O child! O child!--my soul, and not my child!--
Dead art thou, dead!--alack, my child is dead;
And with my child my joys are buried!

Friar.
Peace, ho, for shame! confusion's cure lives not
In these confusions. Heaven and yourself
Had part in this fair maid; now heaven hath all,
And all the better is it for the maid:
Your part in her you could not keep from death;
But heaven keeps his part in eternal life.
The most you sought was her promotion;
For 'twas your heaven she should be advanc'd:
And weep ye now, seeing she is advanc'd
Above the clouds, as high as heaven itself?
O, in this love, you love your child so ill

That you run mad, seeing that she is well:
She's not well married that lives married long:
But she's best married that dies married young.
Dry up your tears, and stick your rosemary
On this fair corse; and, as the custom is,
In all her best array bear her to church;
For though fond nature bids us all lament,
Yet nature's tears are reason's merriment.

Capulet.
All things that we ordained festival
Turn from their office to black funeral:
Our instruments to melancholy bells;
Our wedding cheer to a sad burial feast;
Our solemn hymns to sullen dirges change;
Our bridal flowers serve for a buried corse,
And all things change them to the contrary.

Friar.
Sir, go you in,--and, madam, go with him;--
And go, Sir Paris;--every one prepare
To follow this fair corse unto her grave:
The heavens do lower upon you for some ill;
Move them no more by crossing their high will.

[Exeunt Capulet, Lady Capulet, Paris, and
Friar.]

1 Musician.
Faith, we may put up our pipes and be gone.

Nurse.
Honest good fellows, ah, put up, put up;
For well you know this is a pitiful case.

[Exit.]

1 Musician.
Ay, by my troth, the case may be amended.

[Enter Peter.]

Peter.
Musicians, O, musicians, 'Heart's ease,' 'Heart's ease':
O, an you will have me live, play 'Heart's ease.'

1 Musician.
Why 'Heart's ease'?

Peter.
O, musicians, because my heart itself plays 'My heart is
full of woe': O, play me some merry dump to comfort me.

1 Musician.
Not a dump we: 'tis no time to play now.

Peter.
You will not then?

1 Musician.
No.

Peter.
I will then give it you soundly.

1 Musician.
What will you give us?

Peter.
No money, on my faith; but the gleek,--I will give you the
minstrel.

1 Musician.
Then will I give you the serving-creature.

Peter.
Then will I lay the serving-creature's dagger on your pate.
I will carry no crotchets: I'll re you, I'll fa you: do you note
me?

1 Musician.
An you re us and fa us, you note us.

2 Musician.
Pray you put up your dagger, and put out your wit.

Peter.
Then have at you with my wit! I will dry-beat you with an
iron wit, and put up my iron dagger.--Answer me like men:

'When griping grief the heart doth wound,
  And doleful dumps the mind oppress,
  Then music with her silver sound'--

why 'silver sound'? why 'music with her silver sound'?--
What say you, Simon Catling?

1 Musician.
Marry, sir, because silver hath a sweet sound.

Peter.
Pretty!--What say you, Hugh Rebeck?

2 Musician.
I say 'silver sound' because musicians sound for silver.

Peter.
Pretty too!--What say you, James Soundpost?

3 Musician.
Faith, I know not what to say.

Peter.
O, I cry you mercy; you are the singer: I will say for you.
It is 'music with her silver sound' because musicians have no
gold for sounding:--

'Then music with her silver sound
  With speedy help doth lend redress.'

[Exit.]

1 Musician.
What a pestilent knave is this same!

2 Musician.
Hang him, Jack!--Come, we'll in here; tarry for the mourners, and stay dinner.

[Exeunt]

Glossary:

pennyworths *small portions.*

68

aqua vitae *alcoholic spirits.*

settled *has stopped flowing.*

deflowered by him *having lost her virginity to him.*

confusion's . . . confusions *the solution is not to be found in this uncontrollable grief.*

promotion *advancement in rank.*

she should be advanced *that is, through the socially advantageous marriage to Paris.*

in this love *in your concern for her material and earthly well-being.*

rosemary *evergreen herb which was used as a symbol of remembrance.*

ordained festival *prepared for the wedding festivities.*

lour *scowl or frown upon.*

pitiful case *pitiful state of affairs.*

merry dump *here an oxymoron: a sad tune or song.*

gleek *a gesture of contempt or a rebuke.*

pate *the head, esp. the top of the head.*

carry no crotchets *put up with none of your notions or whims.*

catling *a small lute or fiddle string made out of cat gut.*

prates *talks much and foolishly; chatters.*

rebeck *a three stringed fiddle.*

tarry for *wait for.*

Act V

Scene I. Mantua. A Street

Summary

While in Mantua, Romeo erroneously thinks that his dreams foretell good news. He dreamed that Juliet found him dead but resuscitated him with her kisses. Romeo's servant, Balthasar, then tells Romeo that Juliet has died. Romeo, controlling his anguish, makes plans to go back to Verona. He offers a poor apothecary a large sum of money to illegally sell him poison. Romeo wants to utilize the poison to kill himself and reunite with Juliet in death.

[Enter Romeo.]

Romeo.
If I may trust the flattering eye of sleep,
My dreams presage some joyful news at hand;
My bosom's lord sits lightly in his throne;
And all this day an unaccustom'd spirit
Lifts me above the ground with cheerful thoughts.
I dreamt my lady came and found me dead,--
Strange dream, that gives a dead man leave to think!--
And breath'd such life with kisses in my lips,
That I reviv'd, and was an emperor.
Ah me! how sweet is love itself possess'd,
When but love's shadows are so rich in joy!

[Enter Balthasar.]

News from Verona!--How now, Balthasar?
Dost thou not bring me letters from the friar?
How doth my lady? Is my father well?
How fares my Juliet? that I ask again;
For nothing can be ill if she be well.

Balthasar.
Then she is well, and nothing can be ill:
Her body sleeps in Capel's monument,
And her immortal part with angels lives.
I saw her laid low in her kindred's vault,
And presently took post to tell it you:

O, pardon me for bringing these ill news,
Since you did leave it for my office, sir.

Romeo.
Is it even so? then I defy you, stars!--
Thou know'st my lodging: get me ink and paper,
And hire post-horses. I will hence to-night.

Balthasar.
I do beseech you, sir, have patience:
Your looks are pale and wild, and do import
Some misadventure.

Romeo.
Tush, thou art deceiv'd:
Leave me, and do the thing I bid thee do.
Hast thou no letters to me from the friar?

Balthasar.
No, my good lord.

Romeo.
No matter: get thee gone,
And hire those horses; I'll be with thee straight.

[Exit Balthasar.]

Well, Juliet, I will lie with thee to-night.
Let's see for means;--O mischief, thou art swift
To enter in the thoughts of desperate men!
I do remember an apothecary,--
And hereabouts he dwells,--which late I noted
In tatter'd weeds, with overwhelming brows,
Culling of simples; meagre were his looks,
Sharp misery had worn him to the bones;
And in his needy shop a tortoise hung,
An alligator stuff'd, and other skins
Of ill-shaped fishes; and about his shelves
A beggarly account of empty boxes,
Green earthen pots, bladders, and musty seeds,
Remnants of packthread, and old cakes of roses,
Were thinly scatter'd, to make up a show.
Noting this penury, to myself I said,
An if a man did need a poison now,
Whose sale is present death in Mantua,
Here lives a caitiff wretch would sell it him.
O, this same thought did but forerun my need;
And this same needy man must sell it me.
As I remember, this should be the house:

Being holiday, the beggar's shop is shut.--
What, ho! apothecary!

[Enter Apothecary.]

Apothecary.
Who calls so loud?

Romeo.
Come hither, man.--I see that thou art poor;
Hold, there is forty ducats: let me have
A dram of poison; such soon-speeding gear
As will disperse itself through all the veins
That the life-weary taker mall fall dead;
And that the trunk may be discharg'd of breath
As violently as hasty powder fir'd
Doth hurry from the fatal cannon's womb.

Apothecary.
Such mortal drugs I have; but Mantua's law
Is death to any he that utters them.

Romeo.
Art thou so bare and full of wretchedness
And fear'st to die? famine is in thy cheeks,
Need and oppression starveth in thine eyes,
Contempt and beggary hangs upon thy back,
The world is not thy friend, nor the world's law:
The world affords no law to make thee rich;
Then be not poor, but break it and take this.

Apothecary.
My poverty, but not my will consents.

Romeo.
I pay thy poverty, and not thy will.

Apothecary.
Put this in any liquid thing you will,
And drink it off; and, if you had the strength
Of twenty men, it would despatch you straight.

Romeo.
There is thy gold; worse poison to men's souls,
Doing more murders in this loathsome world
Than these poor compounds that thou mayst not
sell:
I sell thee poison; thou hast sold me none.
Farewell: buy food and get thyself in flesh.--

Come, cordial and not poison, go with me
To Juliet's grave; for there must I use thee.

[Exeunt]

Glossary:

presage *predict; forecast.*

my bosom's lord *love.*

unaccustomed spirit *unusually high spirits.*

**lifts me above the ground with cheerful
thoughts** *Romeo is almost walking on air.*

love's shadows *dreams; visions.*

post-horses *horses kept at a post house, or inn,
for couriers and post chaises or for hire to
travelers.*

weeds *garments; clothing.*

overwhelming *overhanging.*

culling of simples *gathering herbs.*

a beggarly account of empty boxes *empty boxes
of little worth.*

remnants of packthread *remains of strong, thick
thread or twine for tying bundles, packages, and
so on.*

old cakes of roses *dried rose leaves pressed into
cakes.*

penury *extreme poverty.*

caitiff *wretched.*

soon-speeding gear *fast-acting.*

utters *sells.*

cordial *an invigorating medicine that stimulates
the heart.*

Scene II. Friar Lawrence's Cell

Summary:

*Friar Laurence finds out that Friar John, the
courier he sent to Mantua with a letter for
Romeo explaining that Juliet is actually alive,
did not reach him because of an outbreak of the
plague and prevented Friar John from leaving
Verona. Friar Laurence then quickly goes to the
Capulet tomb because it is almost time for Juliet
to awake.*

[Enter Friar John.]

Friar John.
Holy Franciscan friar! brother, ho!

[Enter Friar Lawrence.]

Friar Lawrence.
This same should be the voice of Friar John.
Welcome from Mantua: what says Romeo?
Or, if his mind be writ, give me his letter.

Friar John.
Going to find a barefoot brother out,
One of our order, to associate me,
Here in this city visiting the sick,
And finding him, the searchers of the town,
Suspecting that we both were in a house
Where the infectious pestilence did reign,
Seal'd up the doors, and would not let us forth;
So that my speed to Mantua there was stay'd.

Friar Lawrence.
Who bare my letter, then, to Romeo?

Friar John.
I could not send it,--here it is again,--
Nor get a messenger to bring it thee,
So fearful were they of infection.

Friar Lawrence.
Unhappy fortune! by my brotherhood,
The letter was not nice, but full of charge
Of dear import; and the neglecting it
May do much danger. Friar John, go hence;

71

Get me an iron crow and bring it straight
Unto my cell.

Friar John.
Brother, I'll go and bring it thee.

[Exit.]

Friar Lawrence.
Now must I to the monument alone;
Within this three hours will fair Juliet wake:
She will beshrew me much that Romeo
Hath had no notice of these accidents;
But I will write again to Mantua,
And keep her at my cell till Romeo come;--
Poor living corse, clos'd in a dead man's tomb!

[Exit.]

Glossary:

barefoot brother *another friar.*

to associate me *to accompany me.*

searchers of the town *health officers whose duty it was to view dead bodies and report on the cause of death.*

nice *trivial.*

charge *important matters.*

dear import *of serious concern.*

crow *a crowbar.*

Scene III. A churchyard; in it a Monument belonging to the Capulets.

Summary:

Paris goes to the Capulet tomb to put flowers in Juliet's memory. His page cautions him that someone is approaching so they hide in some bushes outside the tomb. Romeo arrives with Balthasar and breaks into the tomb with the intent of seeing Juliet one last time. Balthasar, fearful about what Romeo is going to do and uneasy of Romeo's wild looks, hides himself outside the tomb as well. Paris, thinking that Romeo has come to defile the bodies in the tomb, confronts Romeo. Romeo attempts to ward Paris off, but Paris challenges Romeo and they fight. Paris is injured and dies. Just before he dies, Paris pleads with Romeo to place him in the tomb next to Juliet. Romeo is filled with sympathy and grants his wish. Paris' page, who has observed the fight, goes to summon the night watchman.

Romeo is astounded by Juliet's beauty even in death. With no hesitation he kisses her, drinks the poison, and dies at her side. An instant later, the Friar arrives and finds the dead bodies of Romeo and Paris. Juliet then wakes up from her death-like sleep and searches for Romeo, saying, "Where is my Romeo?" After seeing the bodies of Romeo and Paris, she decides to remain in the tomb.

The Friar attempts in desperation to persuade Juliet to leave as the night watchman approaches, but Juliet declines. The Friar takes off, and Juliet is by herself with Romeo and Paris dead by her side. She attempts to consume poison from Romeo's vial. After finding the vial empty, she attempts to kiss some poison from his lips. Hearing the night watchman coming near, Juliet fatally stabs herself using Romeo's dagger.

The night watchman as well as the Prince arrives shortly thereafter, accompanied by the Capulets and Lord Montague. Lady Montague has died of anguish at Romeo's expulsion. The Friar faithfully reports the events of the past week and offers his own life as atonement. The Prince recognizes the Friar's compassionate intent but instead puts the blame for the deaths exclusively on Montague and Capulet for their long-lasting dispute. The Prince also finds fault with himself for his leniency and penalizes Montague and Capulet severely. The two families finally resolve their dispute as the Prince ends the play by stating, "For never was a story of more woe / Than this of Juliet and her Romeo."

[Enter Paris, and his Page bearing flowers and a torch.]

Paris.
Give me thy torch, boy: hence, and stand aloof;
Yet put it out, for I would not be seen.
Under yond yew tree lay thee all along,
Holding thine ear close to the hollow ground;
So shall no foot upon the churchyard tread,--
Being loose, unfirm, with digging up of graves,-
But thou shalt hear it: whistle then to me,
As signal that thou hear'st something approach.
Give me those flowers. Do as I bid thee, go.

Page.
[Aside.] I am almost afraid to stand alone
Here in the churchyard; yet I will adventure.

[Retires.]

Paris.
Sweet flower, with flowers thy bridal bed I strew:
  O woe! thy canopy is dust and stones!
Which with sweet water nightly I will dew;
  Or, wanting that, with tears distill'd by moans:
The obsequies that I for thee will keep,
Nightly shall be to strew thy grave and weep.

[The Page whistles.]

The boy gives warning something doth approach.
What cursed foot wanders this way to-night,
To cross my obsequies and true love's rite?
What, with a torch! muffle me, night, awhile.

[Retires.]

[Enter Romeo and Balthasar with a torch, mattock, &c.]

Romeo.
Give me that mattock and the wrenching iron.
Hold, take this letter; early in the morning
See thou deliver it to my lord and father.
Give me the light; upon thy life I charge thee,
Whate'er thou hear'st or seest, stand all aloof
And do not interrupt me in my course.
Why I descend into this bed of death
Is partly to behold my lady's face,
But chiefly to take thence from her dead finger
A precious ring,--a ring that I must use
In dear employment: therefore hence, be gone:--
But if thou, jealous, dost return to pry
In what I further shall intend to do,
By heaven, I will tear thee joint by joint,
And strew this hungry churchyard with thy limbs:
The time and my intents are savage-wild;
More fierce and more inexorable far
Than empty tigers or the roaring sea.

Balthasar.
I will be gone, sir, and not trouble you.

Romeo.
So shalt thou show me friendship.--Take thou that:
Live, and be prosperous: and farewell, good fellow.

Balthasar.
For all this same, I'll hide me hereabout:
His looks I fear, and his intents I doubt.

[Retires.]

Romeo.
Thou detestable maw, thou womb of death,
Gorg'd with the dearest morsel of the earth,
Thus I enforce thy rotten jaws to open,

[Breaking open the door of the monument.]

And, in despite, I'll cram thee with more food!

Paris.
This is that banish'd haughty Montague
That murder'd my love's cousin,--with which grief,
It is supposed, the fair creature died,--

And here is come to do some villanous shame
To the dead bodies: I will apprehend him.--

[Advances.]

Stop thy unhallow'd toil, vile Montague!
Can vengeance be pursu'd further than death?
Condemned villain, I do apprehend thee;
Obey, and go with me; for thou must die.

Romeo.
I must indeed; and therefore came I hither.--
Good gentle youth, tempt not a desperate man;
Fly hence and leave me:--think upon these gone;
Let them affright thee.--I beseech thee, youth,
Put not another sin upon my head
By urging me to fury: O, be gone!
By heaven, I love thee better than myself;
For I come hither arm'd against myself:
Stay not, be gone;--live, and hereafter say,
A madman's mercy bid thee run away.

Paris.
I do defy thy conjurations,
And apprehend thee for a felon here.

Romeo.
Wilt thou provoke me? then have at thee, boy!

[They fight.]

Page.
O lord, they fight! I will go call the watch.

[Exit.]

Paris.
O, I am slain! [Falls.] If thou be merciful,
Open the tomb, lay me with Juliet.

[Dies.]

Romeo.
In faith, I will.--Let me peruse this face:--
Mercutio's kinsman, noble County Paris!--
What said my man, when my betossed soul
Did not attend him as we rode? I think
He told me Paris should have married Juliet:
Said he not so? or did I dream it so?
Or am I mad, hearing him talk of Juliet,

To think it was so?--O, give me thy hand,
One writ with me in sour misfortune's book!
I'll bury thee in a triumphant grave;--
A grave? O, no, a lanthorn, slaught'red youth,
For here lies Juliet, and her beauty makes
This vault a feasting presence full of light.
Death, lie thou there, by a dead man interr'd.

[Laying Paris in the monument.]

How oft when men are at the point of death
Have they been merry! which their keepers call
A lightning before death: O, how may I
Call this a lightning?--O my love! my wife!
Death, that hath suck'd the honey of thy breath,
Hath had no power yet upon thy beauty:
Thou art not conquer'd; beauty's ensign yet
Is crimson in thy lips and in thy cheeks,
And death's pale flag is not advanced there.--
Tybalt, liest thou there in thy bloody sheet?
O, what more favour can I do to thee
Than with that hand that cut thy youth in twain
To sunder his that was thine enemy?
Forgive me, cousin!--Ah, dear Juliet,
Why art thou yet so fair? Shall I believe
That unsubstantial death is amorous;
And that the lean abhorred monster keeps
Thee here in dark to be his paramour?
For fear of that I still will stay with thee,
And never from this palace of dim night
Depart again: here, here will I remain
With worms that are thy chambermaids: O, here
Will I set up my everlasting rest;
And shake the yoke of inauspicious stars
From this world-wearied flesh.--Eyes, look your
last!
Arms, take your last embrace! and, lips, O you
The doors of breath, seal with a righteous kiss
A dateless bargain to engrossing death!--
Come, bitter conduct, come, unsavoury guide!
Thou desperate pilot, now at once run on
The dashing rocks thy sea-sick weary bark!
Here's to my love! [Drinks.]--O true apothecary!
Thy drugs are quick.--Thus with a kiss I die.

[Dies.]

[Enter, at the other end of the Churchyard, Friar
Lawrence, with a lantern, crow, and spade.]

74

Friar.
Saint Francis be my speed! how oft to-night
Have my old feet stumbled at graves!--Who's
there?
Who is it that consorts, so late, the dead?

Balthasar.
Here's one, a friend, and one that knows you
well.

Friar.
Bliss be upon you! Tell me, good my friend,
What torch is yond that vainly lends his light
To grubs and eyeless skulls? as I discern,
It burneth in the Capels' monument.

Balthasar.
It doth so, holy sir; and there's my master,
One that you love.

Friar.
Who is it?

Balthasar.
Romeo.

Friar.
How long hath he been there?

Balthasar.
Full half an hour.

Friar.
Go with me to the vault.

Balthasar.
I dare not, sir;
My master knows not but I am gone hence;
And fearfully did menace me with death
If I did stay to look on his intents.

Friar.
Stay then; I'll go alone:--fear comes upon me;
O, much I fear some ill unlucky thing.

Balthasar.
As I did sleep under this yew tree here,
I dreamt my master and another fought,
And that my master slew him.

Friar.
Romeo! [Advances.]
Alack, alack! what blood is this which stains
The stony entrance of this sepulchre?--
What mean these masterless and gory swords
To lie discolour'd by this place of peace?

[Enters the monument.]

Romeo! O, pale!--Who else? what, Paris too?
And steep'd in blood?--Ah, what an unkind hour
Is guilty of this lamentable chance!--The lady
stirs.

[Juliet wakes and stirs.]

Juliet.
O comfortable friar! where is my lord?--
I do remember well where I should be,
And there I am:--where is my Romeo?

[Noise within.]

Friar.
I hear some noise.--Lady, come from that nest
Of death, contagion, and unnatural sleep:
A greater power than we can contradict
Hath thwarted our intents:--come, come away!
Thy husband in thy bosom there lies dead;
And Paris too:--come, I'll dispose of thee
Among a sisterhood of holy nuns:
Stay not to question, for the watch is coming.
Come, go, good Juliet [noise within],--I dare no
longer stay.

Juliet.
Go, get thee hence, for I will not away.--

[Exit Friar Lawrence.]

What's here? a cup, clos'd in my true love's
hand?
Poison, I see, hath been his timeless end:--
O churl! drink all, and left no friendly drop
To help me after?--I will kiss thy lips;
Haply some poison yet doth hang on them,
To make me die with a restorative.

[Kisses him.]

Thy lips are warm!

1 Watch.
[Within.] Lead, boy:--which way?

Juliet.
Yea, noise?--Then I'll be brief.--O happy
dagger!

[Snatching Romeo's dagger.]

This is thy sheath [stabs herself]; there rest, and
let me die.

[Falls on Romeo's body and dies.]

[Enter Watch, with the Page of Paris.]

Page.
This is the place; there, where the torch doth
burn.

1 Watch.
The ground is bloody; search about the
churchyard:
Go, some of you, whoe'er you find attach.

[Exeunt some of the Watch.]

Pitiful sight! here lies the county slain;--
And Juliet bleeding; warm, and newly dead,
Who here hath lain this two days buried.--
Go, tell the prince;--run to the Capulets,--
Raise up the Montagues,--some others search:--

[Exeunt others of the Watch.]

We see the ground whereon these woes do lie;
But the true ground of all these piteous woes
We cannot without circumstance descry.

[Re-enter some of the Watch with Balthasar.]

2 Watch.
Here's Romeo's man; we found him in the
churchyard.

1 Watch.
Hold him in safety till the prince come hither.

[Re-enter others of the Watch with Friar
Lawrence.]

3 Watch.
Here is a friar, that trembles, sighs, and weeps:
We took this mattock and this spade from him
As he was coming from this churchyard side.

1 Watch.
A great suspicion: stay the friar too.

[Enter the Prince and Attendants.]

Prince.
What misadventure is so early up,
That calls our person from our morning's rest?

[Enter Capulet, Lady Capulet, and others.]

Capulet.
What should it be, that they so shriek abroad?

Lady Capulet.
The people in the street cry Romeo,
Some Juliet, and some Paris; and all run,
With open outcry, toward our monument.

Prince.
What fear is this which startles in our ears?

1 Watch.
Sovereign, here lies the County Paris slain;
And Romeo dead; and Juliet, dead before,
Warm and new kill'd.

Prince.
Search, seek, and know how this foul murder
comes.

1 Watch.
Here is a friar, and slaughter'd Romeo's man,
With instruments upon them fit to open
These dead men's tombs.

Capulet.
O heaven!--O wife, look how our daughter
bleeds!
This dagger hath mista'en,--for, lo, his house

Is empty on the back of Montague,--
And it mis-sheathed in my daughter's bosom!

Lady Capulet.
O me! this sight of death is as a bell
That warns my old age to a sepulchre.

[Enter Montague and others.]

Prince.
Come, Montague; for thou art early up,
To see thy son and heir more early down.

Montague.
Alas, my liege, my wife is dead to-night;
Grief of my son's exile hath stopp'd her breath:
What further woe conspires against mine age?

Prince.
Look, and thou shalt see.

Montague.
O thou untaught! what manners is in this,
To press before thy father to a grave?

Prince.
Seal up the mouth of outrage for a while,
Till we can clear these ambiguities,
And know their spring, their head, their true
descent;
And then will I be general of your woes,
And lead you even to death: meantime forbear,
And let mischance be slave to patience.--
Bring forth the parties of suspicion.

Friar.
I am the greatest, able to do least,
Yet most suspected, as the time and place
Doth make against me, of this direful murder;
And here I stand, both to impeach and purge
Myself condemned and myself excus'd.

Prince.
Then say at once what thou dost know in this.

Friar.
I will be brief, for my short date of breath
Is not so long as is a tedious tale.
Romeo, there dead, was husband to that Juliet;
And she, there dead, that Romeo's faithful wife:

I married them; and their stol'n marriage day
Was Tybalt's doomsday, whose untimely death
Banish'd the new-made bridegroom from this
city;
For whom, and not for Tybalt, Juliet pin'd.
You, to remove that siege of grief from her,
Betroth'd, and would have married her perforce,
To County Paris:--then comes she to me,
And with wild looks, bid me devise some means
To rid her from this second marriage,
Or in my cell there would she kill herself.
Then gave I her, so tutored by my art,
A sleeping potion; which so took effect
As I intended, for it wrought on her
The form of death: meantime I writ to Romeo
That he should hither come as this dire night,
To help to take her from her borrow'd grave,
Being the time the potion's force should cease.
But he which bore my letter, Friar John,
Was stay'd by accident; and yesternight
Return'd my letter back. Then all alone
At the prefixed hour of her waking
Came I to take her from her kindred's vault;
Meaning to keep her closely at my cell
Till I conveniently could send to Romeo:
But when I came,--some minute ere the time
Of her awaking,--here untimely lay
The noble Paris and true Romeo dead.
She wakes; and I entreated her come forth
And bear this work of heaven with patience:
But then a noise did scare me from the tomb;
And she, too desperate, would not go with me,
But, as it seems, did violence on herself.
All this I know; and to the marriage
Her nurse is privy: and if ought in this
Miscarried by my fault, let my old life
Be sacrific'd, some hour before his time,
Unto the rigour of severest law.

Prince.
We still have known thee for a holy man.--
Where's Romeo's man? what can he say in this?

Balthasar.
I brought my master news of Juliet's death;
And then in post he came from Mantua
To this same place, to this same monument.
This letter he early bid me give his father;
And threaten'd me with death, going in the vault,
If I departed not, and left him there.

Prince.
Give me the letter,--I will look on it.--
Where is the county's page that rais'd the
watch?--
Sirrah, what made your master in this place?

Boy.
He came with flowers to strew his lady's grave;
And bid me stand aloof, and so I did:
Anon comes one with light to ope the tomb;
And by-and-by my master drew on him;
And then I ran away to call the watch.

Prince.
This letter doth make good the friar's words,
Their course of love, the tidings of her death:
And here he writes that he did buy a poison
Of a poor 'pothecary, and therewithal
Came to this vault to die, and lie with Juliet.--
Where be these enemies?--Capulet,--Montague,-
See what a scourge is laid upon your hate,
That heaven finds means to kill your joys with
love!
And I, for winking at your discords too,
Have lost a brace of kinsmen:--all are punish'd.

Capulet.
O brother Montague, give me thy hand:
This is my daughter's jointure, for no more
Can I demand.

Montague.
But I can give thee more:
For I will raise her statue in pure gold;
That while Verona by that name is known,
There shall no figure at such rate be set
As that of true and faithful Juliet.

Capulet.
As rich shall Romeo's by his lady's lie;
Poor sacrifices of our enmity!

Prince.
A glooming peace this morning with it brings;
    The sun for sorrow will not show his head.
Go hence, to have more talk of these sad things;
    Some shall be pardon'd, and some punished;
For never was a story of more woe
Than this of Juliet and her Romeo.

[Exeunt.]

Glossary:

obsequies *funeral rites.*

cross *to thwart.*

mattock *a tool for loosening the soil: it is like a
pickax but has a flat, adz-shaped blade on one
or both sides.*

dear employment *important purpose.*

jealous *suspicious.*

conjuration *solemn entreaty.*

lantern *an open or windowed structure on the
roof of a building or in the upper part of a tower
or the like, to admit light or air.*

feasting presence *presence chamber: the room
in which a king or other person of rank or
distinction formally receives guests.*

keepers *guards, as of prisoners.*

a light'ning before death! *Romeo refers to the
belief that on the point of death the spirits were
supposed to revive.*

conduct *that is, the poison.*

unthrifty *unlucky.*

discoloured *bloodstained.*

churl *a surly, ill-bred person.*

rust *corruption, decay.*

descry *detect.*

let mischance be slave to patience *submit to
these unfortunate events with patience.*

kill your joys *kill your children and turn your
joy to sorrow.*
winking *turning a blind eye to.*

glooming peace *peace overshadowed with grief.*

Made in the USA
Middletown, DE
02 January 2020